CHRISTMAS PAST

THE WITCHES OF MINGUS MOUNTAIN - BOOK 6

CHRISTINE POPE

DARK VALENTINE
PRESS

CHRISTMAS PAST

Copyright © 2025 by Christine Pope

ISBN: 978-1-946435-89-7

Published by Dark Valentine Press

Cover design by Indie Author Services

Ebook formatting by Indie Author Services

1

On that Wednesday afternoon in mid-December, the Asylum restaurant in Jerome's Grand Hotel was nearly deserted.

Which was the exact reason why my fiancé Seth McAllister and I had gone there to finalize the menu and the guest list for the reception, to look over the place and compare it to the notes and photos we'd gotten from the florist to make sure that everything was going to line up the way we planned and that there weren't any last-minute additions or subtractions we needed to make.

After Seth had asked me to marry him almost six months earlier, we'd sat down and discussed exactly what we wanted for a wedding. I'd never been the kind of girl to dream about an extravagant event with ten bridesmaids and dove releases and all the other expensive craziness those sorts of ceremonies generally involved.

To be honest, thanks to my crazy time-traveling magical talent, I hadn't been sure whether I'd ever find anyone who would put up with me, so it had seemed better to think small and not have too many expectations.

But Seth's and my adventures in time had bonded us in a way I'd never imagined possible, and once we'd safely landed back in the mid-twenty-first century…my time, even if it hadn't originally been his…it had pretty much been a foregone conclusion that we would spend the rest of our lives together.

At any rate, we'd both agreed that we wanted to get married in Jerome; he was a McAllister, and his witch clan's roots went way back here. The crazy little town had become my adopted home as well, even though I was a Wilcox from Flagstaff and had spent my whole life there until recently.

The McAllisters of the present day were his family, too, of course, but his immediate family— his mother and father and older brother Charles —had remained behind in 1926. That was when I'd first met Seth, confused and frightened and not realizing at first exactly how far back in time I'd fallen after I tripped and blacked out in the abandoned mine shaft high above the town.

That was all behind us now, however. I didn't

want to think about the past anymore. No, I just wanted to focus on the future...our future together.

To justify taking up a table at the Asylum, Seth and I had both ordered a glass of wine and an appetizer. A huge Christmas tree glittered in the foyer, and faux pine boughs wrapped with red velvet ribbons decorated the paintings that hung on the main dining room's wood-paneled walls. Down the hill in the bungalow the two of us shared—he'd owned the house back in 1926 and the current owner, my cousin Margot, had been kind enough to return it to him—we had similar decorations up, although we'd decided against a tree, since we weren't going to be around much to enjoy it.

The guest list lay on the table in front of Seth, next to the menu for the reception banquet. We'd already agreed that the event should be small and intimate, just my immediate family from Flagstaff and the McAllister cousins we were both close to —my friend Bellamy and her fiancé Marc Trujillo, Brianna McAllister and her significant other, Bill Garrett...who wasn't quite as human as he looked...along with the clan elders and people like Rachel McAllister, who'd owned the mercantile Seth and I now ran and had turned out to be his long-lost great-niece.

Or was it great-niece, once removed?

This sort of stuff could get awfully complicated when you were dealing with time travel and connections that spanned generations.

All in all, about forty people had been invited. The Asylum honestly wouldn't accommodate much more than that anyway, which was part of the reason why Seth and I had decided on the restaurant as the venue for both the ceremony and the reception to follow. I knew that Bellamy was planning a big wedding in the spring at the winery she and Marc had bought with her lottery winnings, and I assumed Bree would have a similarly large event at some point, although when asked, she only smiled and said that she and "Bill" —aka Belshegar—were still talking about it but hadn't hammered out all the details yet.

My mother had tried to gently suggest that Seth and I should have our wedding in Flagstaff, where my cousin Lucas had already offered the reception space at the fancy country club he belonged to, but I'd shot that idea down immediately. Seth was already so far away from the world and the people he'd known that I'd understood from the beginning that we needed to have the wedding in Jerome.

It was my adopted hometown, too, and getting married anywhere else just didn't make sense.

Now, though, Seth pushed the guest list aside

as he reached for his glass of Mule's Mistake, one of our favorite local wines, and I found myself frowning.

"Everything okay?"

At once, the corners of his mouth turned up. "Sure."

That smile might have fooled some people, but it didn't fool me. I saw how it didn't reach his clear blue eyes, how something about his gaze seemed very far away.

I still thought he was the handsomest man in the world, with his chiseled, boyish features and thick brown hair...but I could also tell when he was trying to hide something from me.

"Seth."

His gaze moved away from mine, toward the snow-dusted streets of Jerome far below us. The Grand Hotel occupied one of the highest points in town, and the views it offered were spectacular. Snow had fallen the night before, just enough to make the settlement seem like something out of a holiday card, and I hoped it would snow again right around the wedding. Not enough to make travel difficult for anyone, of course, but just the right amount to ensure Jerome looked as magical as I knew it truly was.

What other word could you use for a town that had been a witch clan's home base for more than a hundred and fifty years?

"Everything looks wonderful," he said at length, then lifted the glass of wine to his lips so he could take a sip. "I'm really glad we're having the wedding here."

"But...?" I probed, and he released a breath before he put the glass back down next to the little plate that held his half-eaten tomato basil bruschetta.

For a long moment, he was silent. Whenever he got like this, I knew he'd probably been wrestling with whatever the issue was for quite a while. We'd had very few hiccups in our relationship, but every once in a while, we hit a bump. Only to be expected, obviously...I didn't care how perfect a relationship was, sometimes things just weren't perfectly smooth...but I knew he didn't want to have any kind of conflict at all because that would force him to admit that he'd left his support system behind. The current-day McAllisters had welcomed him with open arms—obviously, because they were still his relatives, even if separated by generations—but it wasn't the same as having his parents around, or the people who'd been his friends since childhood.

"It's okay," I said quietly. Only two other couples occupied the restaurant at this odd hour of the afternoon, and holiday music drifted from the speakers placed strategically around the room, so I doubted anyone could hear us. Still, I wanted to keep this conversation to ourselves, for obvious reasons. "You know you can tell me anything."

Seth's gaze met mine for a moment. I saw the sadness in his eyes, although I didn't think it was because of anything I'd said or done.

"The wedding is going to be perfect," he replied. "And I like this venue a lot. It's definitely the best place in Jerome for this kind of gathering."

"But...?" I said again.

His fingers played with the stem of his wine glass, although he didn't seem inclined to pick it up. "But I still hate the idea that my parents never knew what happened to me. To everyone in that time, I just vanished into thin air."

That was definitely the most troubling aspect of our situation. It was true that when we'd left Jerome on that hot June afternoon in 1926, the only person who had even an inkling of what was going on was Seth's older brother Charles. The two of them had been at odds over Charles's involvement in a local bootlegging ring, although Charles had made noises about giving it up... mainly because he'd just become the consort of the clan's *prima*-in-waiting, Abigail McAllister. Still, Seth had gotten caught up in the whole mess, and the leader of the local bootleggers had managed to shoot me in the stomach.

Not a pleasant moment, although a combination of my erratic time-traveling talent and Seth's gift for teleportation had taken us away to 1884 Flagstaff, where one of my distant ancestors, the clan's healer at the time, had managed to patch me up. No harm, no foul.

But although we'd visited Jerome again in the late 1940s—purely by accident, since I was only trying to get us home to the twenty-first century —and therefore Charles knew something of what had happened to us, Seth's parents had no idea what had become of their younger son, since they'd passed away by then. The newspapers from June 1926 claimed that he'd died in a fall at one of the mines...not so rare an occurrence in the rough-and-tumble mining town the place had been at the time...and although Henry and Molly McAllister had probably known Seth hadn't perished in that particular fashion, they still could have had no real idea of what had happened to him.

"I know," I said. "It would have been nice if that Collector jerk had dropped an artifact that allows us to send messages through time, but that sure didn't happen."

The Collector...none of us knew his real name, or even what he truly looked like, since the times he'd appeared in Jerome he'd been wearing a magical disguise...seemed hell-bent on gathering as many enchanted artifacts and talismans as he could. Seth and I had found one such object back in 1884 Flagstaff and had brought it forward in time with us. While I still thought we'd done the right thing, since it had been in the hands of a warlock who was using it to enhance his powers in a very public way, I also had to acknowledge that if I'd never brought the amulet here, then the Collector would probably have had no reason to turn his attention toward our tiny town.

Well, done was done, and we'd just have to deal with the aftermath as best we could. At least it seemed as if he'd been banished for the time being, thanks to the combined magic of Angela and Connor, the McAllister *prima* and the Wilcox *primus,* and the clan elders…along with a very welcome assist from Brianna McAllister and her significant other, Bill.

But because we certainly didn't have access to the Collector's cache of rare, magical objects, there was no way to send a message back in time to Seth's parents to let them know he was happy and healthy and thriving.

An idea popped into my mind, one so outrageous, I knew I should just push it away and ignore it. We were safe here now, and the last thing I should be doing with our wedding only ten days away was to start stirring the pot.

"What is it?" Seth asked. He was frowning a little, but I thought that was probably because he knew what to expect when I got that kind of look on my face.

The same look that had gotten us into trouble more than once.

"Maybe we should go back and tell them," I said, and Seth stared at me in consternation.

"Go back to 1926?"

I nodded.

"That's impossible," he replied. When his tone turned flat like that, I knew he was getting ready to dig his heels in.

But because I'd been expecting that kind of reaction, I refused to let myself get too discouraged.

"Why not?" I said. "It's not like we haven't traveled in time before."

Seth paused then, his gaze quickly moving around the room, as if to make sure we couldn't be overheard. But the other two couples in the dining room looked absorbed in their conversations, and it seemed pretty clear that they weren't paying any attention to us.

"We did," he replied, pitching his voice low so it couldn't be overheard. "Without any real control, and with a lot of personal risk. Have you forgotten that the only reason we were able to get back here at all was because of the amulet and Ruby McAllister giving us a magical boost?"

No, I hadn't forgotten. The amulet had been

made by a long-ago warlock and possessed the ability to strengthen the magical gifts of whoever held it. Even with it beefing up my time-travel talent, I still wouldn't have had the ability to send Seth and me forward nearly a hundred years if it hadn't been for Ruby joining her strength to ours and catapulting us forward in time.

But I'd been practicing these past few months. Not traveling that far, of course, but sending myself forward and backward a day here, a week there. All those jumps had worked flawlessly, which seemed to be a clear signal that I was starting to finally get some control over a talent I'd once looked upon as not much more than a liability. My other talent, the one I'd inherited from my father and which allowed me to conceal my witch nature, had come in much more handy during Seth's and my travels in time.

I hadn't told Seth about my little experiments, mostly because I knew he'd think I was taking unnecessary risks when everything seemed calm and settled, and there was no reason for me to be anywhere except where...and when...I currently was.

Now, though...now it sure seemed as if I had a very good reason to put my recently honed skills to the test.

"No," I told him. "But I really think I can do this. I've been practicing."

At once, he sat up straighter, and those clear blue eyes might as well have been lasers boring right through me. "You've *what?*"

The last syllable came out louder than he'd probably intended, and he sent a worried look around before seeming to decide that no one else appeared to have noticed the minor outburst.

"I've been practicing," I said quietly. "Nothing big, but it's been enough to prove to myself that my control over my gift is a lot better than it once was. For all I know, the exposure to the amulet helped permanently strengthen something about it, or maybe it was something about entwining my powers with Ruby's to get us back to the current day. Anyway, I really think we can go back to 1926 without too much trouble. Wouldn't you like that? Don't you want to have another Christmas with your family, one where, even if you don't want to tell them exactly what happened, you could at least let them know that you're safe and everything is all right?"

Another long pause, one during which I could see the way Seth swallowed, the way his eyes couldn't quite meet mine. In that moment, I saw how badly he wanted to go...and how much he wrestled with himself for entertaining the notion...if even for a second or two.

Then he said, his tone flat again, "It's too big a risk."

"You don't know that for sure," I replied.

Now he did look directly at me, and the worry in his face was so clear, I guessed even the people sitting across the room could have picked it up.

Luckily, they still weren't paying any attention to us.

"Why didn't you tell me you were practicing?"

The words were spoken simply, without a hint of accusation. He didn't seem to be angry, just worried.

"Because I didn't want to upset you," I said. "And I was doing very small jumps, the kind that wouldn't have caused much of a problem even if I'd gotten stuck when I landed. That didn't happen, though. So I know I have a lot more control now than I did even six months ago."

Because he didn't say anything right away, I knew he was wrestling with his thoughts, coming up with all the reasons why this was a crazy idea… and doing his best to ignore the ones, maybe stronger, that were telling him he should go back to give his parents some peace of mind.

When he spoke, I could tell he'd already made the decision but wasn't going to voice it out loud until he'd hammered out a few pertinent points.

"How do you plan to do this?" he asked. "Because if we just appear in the middle of the mercantile, people are going to ask questions."

"Not a problem," I said calmly. "We can use

the old mine shaft to come and go—it wasn't in use even in 1926, so we shouldn't bump into anyone there. And we can try to find some period-correct clothes in the vintage shop in Cotton-wood, but if they don't have anything that'll work, then I'll see what I can find on eBay and Etsy and find out if they can overnight it here."

Too bad we hadn't departed from the 1920s during our last time jump, or I wouldn't have had to worry about clothes at all. However, since we'd come here from 1947, those outfits wouldn't work. We'd hung onto them and gone to a couple of vintage dances in Prescott—it turned out that Seth picked up swing and the Lindy hop pretty quickly—but they'd be just as out of place in 1926 Jerome as they were in the present day.

Maybe more so, since at least in our current time, vintage clothing seemed to be a style choice that never went completely away.

Now Seth was smiling just a little. "It sounds like you've thought of everything."

"I don't know about 'everything,'" I said. "But I really think we can make this work. And because we're moving around in time, we have all the flexibility in the world. We can go to Christmas in 1926 and be back here for our own celebration without anyone noticing."

At least, that was the optimal scenario. If I really screwed up, I might not be able to pinpoint things exactly. Missing our wedding would be the worst outcome, of course, but there was also the rehearsal dinner and Christmas Eve at my parents' house, and all the million and one social commitments that always cropped up during the holidays.

One good thing was that Seth and I had hired extra help—well, a bunch of McAllister cousins—to watch the store, so there wouldn't be too much problem about us being MIA at the height of the busiest shopping season. And Rachel had also volunteered to check in and make sure everything was running smoothly. She'd officially retired after she handed over the reins of McAllister Mercantile to Seth and me, but I knew she'd be only too happy to lend her expertise if necessary.

As far as I could tell, we had all the bases covered. The only thing that remained was the go-ahead from Seth.

He seemed to still be pondering my plan about buying a vintage wardrobe for our trip in time. Sure, it would be expensive, but we had the money. The store was doing well, the bungalow had been paid off for more than a hundred years, and everyone in our respective witch clans got a monthly stipend to help pad things. Dropping even a grand on getting us outfitted wouldn't begin to make a dent.

"It'll be fun," I said, and reached across the table so I could place my hand on top of his.

Months had passed since he'd last worked in the mines, but those fingers were still as strong as ever and slightly callused, probably from all the hauling and stacking he did in the store's stockroom.

A reluctant grin plucked at his lips. "I didn't think it was about 'fun,'" he said. "I thought it was about getting some closure with my parents."

"Well, that, too," I allowed. "But when I was in 1926, it was summer, and hot without a single air conditioner in sight. I'd like to experience past Jerome at Christmas and see if it was as magical then as it is now."

He shifted his hand slightly so he could entwine his fingers with mine. "Oh, it'll be magical," he said.

"Does that mean we're going?"

A silence again, although he didn't try to pull his hand away. If anything, his fingers tightened a little—not enough to hurt, of course, but just enough to signal that he had no intention of letting go.

"Yes," he said, and his voice was almost heavy. "I need to do this."

I smiled across the table at him…and also sent out a little prayer to the universe that this Christmas adventure would work out the way we'd planned.

2

Seth would be the first to admit that he still didn't understand all the ins and outs of online shopping—he much preferred to go to stores in person to get what he needed, whether that was down the hill in Cottonwood or over the mountain to Prescott, which had many more shops—but his time with Devynn had taught him that she was an expert at it.

Only two days after their conversation at The Asylum, a number of boxes appeared on the front porch of their bungalow. Since it was the holiday season and they were planning a Christmas wedding as well, he doubted anyone would think twice about the arrival of all those parcels.

Well, as long as they didn't see what was inside.

A suit for him and a pair of wool trousers,

along with shirts and ties, shoes and underthings. It looked as if Devynn wanted to make sure they had enough for a stay of a few days, although their plan was only to be there Christmas Eve and part of Christmas Day, and then come straight back to the twenty-first century. Still, after the way she'd been stranded in 1926 for weeks and the two of them in 1884 Flagstaff for just as long, he supposed it was wise to have some contingencies set in place.

Just in case.

And Devynn had decided it would be good to leave on the solstice, mainly because she thought the extra energy of the day might be just what they needed to land in the correct place and time. Because that decision had only delayed their departure by a day, Seth wasn't too worried about it…even as he wondered if there was any true merit to the scheme, or whether she was just hoping the shift from dark to light would help them with their journey back to 1926.

She'd told everyone they were going down to Scottsdale for the weekend so she could get some spa treatments, and no one had even blinked at the story. Possibly, all brides went to get massages and facials and whatever else went on in those sorts of places, because all anyone said was that they hoped the two of them would have a good time.

Night fell on the evening of the solstice, and Seth and Devynn got into the antique clothing she'd been able to locate online. The suit and shoes and everything else fit him better than he'd expected, but when he asked her about it, she only smiled.

"I already had all your measurements because of getting you fitted for your wedding suit," she explained when they met in the living room, the remainder of their vintage wardrobe stowed in a large leather suitcase, also an antique. "So it was easy enough to plug those in when I was looking for stuff online. But I'm glad it all fits so well— not everyone selling online is an expert at measuring stuff, so it can still be something of a crap shoot."

Seth brushed his hand against the lapel of his jacket. "Well, it sure looks like you keep rolling sevens."

She smiled. He still wasn't sure how she'd done it, but somehow she'd managed to curl her long brown hair—which usually hung to mid-back— and arrange it with careful pins so it made a good approximation of the bobbed hairstyles that had been popular in his day. Not with everyone, of course...his mother had worn hers in a bun, because she would have rather walked down Main Street in her underthings than cut off her hair...

but still, a lot of his cousins had shorn their long locks.

With her hair styled this way, and wearing a pretty dark green dress she'd found online, Devynn should fit right in.

They put on their overcoats and hats, also vintage finds, and Seth bent down to pick up the suitcase. Because they were only bringing clothing for a few days, it hadn't been necessary to pack more than one.

"Ready?" Devynn asked.

Was he? Even now, it seemed mildly insane that he'd agreed to such a venture. Although he wanted his parents to know the truth and not go to their graves worrying about him, he also knew he and Devynn were taking an enormous risk, no matter how much she wanted to protest that all her practicing had practically guaranteed the safety of such a trip.

What if they got trapped in the past forever? At least they would be together, but she would be leaving all her friends and family behind. Some might have argued he'd done that very thing, and yet he knew the situation was different. They'd discussed the matter in depth, and he'd concluded that he would rather travel into the future than have her remain in the past. It had been a conscious decision.

If something went wrong now, she wouldn't be able to make that kind of choice.

But her big, blue-gray eyes were shining, and her lovely mouth with its coating of dark red lipstick had turned up at the corners. She certainly didn't seem to be harboring any doubts, or if she were, she was doing a very good job of hiding them.

If he backed out now, he would look like a coward.

His hands took her gloved ones, slender but strong under the kidskin.

"I'm ready," he said.

They'd agreed to jump to the abandoned mine shaft at around four-thirty in the afternoon. Seth knew the crews ended their day at four at this time of year, since dark came so early. Devynn had agreed that it sounded like a good idea, since the last thing either of them wanted was for anyone to observe their arrival. True, the mine shaft had been an exploratory one, something that had been pretty much ignored after the surveyors discovered it didn't possess any significant veins of copper or silver, but they still couldn't take the chance of being spotted as they appeared out of nowhere.

Especially since the shaft had also been used

by the local bootlegging crew, although Seth had to hope they'd moved their operations elsewhere after the local ringleader, Lionel Allenby, had met his fate at the bottom of a nearby cliff. Everyone thought it had been an accidental death, but the bootleggers themselves most likely had a different opinion as to what had really happened.

Sudden, violent death was just part of the deal.

The air was cold when they appeared in the shaft, colder than the day they'd left behind them in the twenty-first century. Devynn pulled her fur-collared coat more closely around her as she studied their surroundings.

"Well, we're in the right place," she announced, since that much was obvious. "I suppose now the real trick is figuring out if we're in the right time."

"Easy enough," Seth said. "Or at least, something we'll find out soon enough if we start walking."

She nodded, and they made their way out of the shaft and along the rough path that led down to the highway. Not for the first time, he found himself wishing that his talent was just a little stronger so he could teleport himself and Devynn to their destination rather than having to trudge along the roadside. But although he could go wherever he wished—and carry roughly forty or fifty pounds while doing so—a full-grown woman was just a bit more than his magical translocation gift allowed.

A car was coming up behind them, and they paused. For some reason, Seth found himself tensing, even though he knew there was no real reason to be worried. The highway was the main route between the Verde Valley and Prescott, the town that had once been Arizona's capital, and people came and went this way all the time.

Of course, if the person in the vehicle was a McAllister, then he and Devynn might have to launch into explanations much earlier than they'd planned.

The car came to a stop. It was a shiny black Ford, several years newer than the Dodge convertible he'd loved so much and had been forced to leave behind in 1926. Still, he recognized the vehicle as a 1925 model, which told him they must have landed fairly close to their target.

And then the passenger-side window rolled down—slowly, and with a fit here and a start there, so different from the smooth, electronically controlled windows of the era he now called home—and a woman peered out. She seemed to be around thirty, pretty, with hair marcelled into pale waves and lipstick nearly the same dark brick shade as Devynn's coating her lips.

She was also an utter stranger, and Seth couldn't help being relieved.

"Need a ride?" she asked. "My husband and I didn't think anyone should be walking in this cold."

Yes, it was very chilly, probably just below freezing. Snow gleamed pale on the roadside, signaling that a storm had come through here recently, although the drifts weren't deep enough to have made their way overly difficult.

"That would be wonderful," he replied. "We're just going to Jerome—McAllister Mercantile."

"It's right on our way," the woman said, and her blue eyes twinkled. "Doing some last-minute Christmas shopping?"

"Something like that," Devynn put in. "We were driving from Prescott, but our car broke down about a mile or so back."

Now the woman's expression turned puzzled. "It did? Milo and I didn't see any cars on the roadway."

"Oh, we pushed it off the road so it wouldn't cause a hazard," Seth said hastily. "But a ride down into Jerome would be wonderful."

The woman nodded. "Then get in."

Seth opened the rear passenger door and helped Devynn negotiate her way inside. She scooched over to seat herself behind the driver, a big, burly man who looked to be about ten years older than his wife.

If she was even his wife at all. He thought it was probably better not to ask.

The important thing was that they wouldn't have to trudge all the way down to Main Street. Devynn had made sure to get shoes with practical heels, so Seth knew she could have made the trek if necessary, but this was much easier.

What had seemed like a daunting walk took only about five minutes. Although he guessed it must be past five o'clock by that point and the mercantile was closed, he knew they didn't have to worry about that, not when it would be easy enough to go around to the back door and let themselves in that way.

The car came to a stop across the street from the shop, and the blonde woman sent them a worried glance over her shoulder. "Oh, dear—it looks as if the mercantile isn't open."

"It's fine," Seth assured her. "My folks own the store, so we'll be going in the back entrance to the apartment."

Now she looked puzzled, as if she couldn't quite figure out why they hadn't corrected her comment about Christmas shopping when it seemed apparent they had an entirely different reason for going to the mercantile. But then her expression cleared, and she shrugged the slightest bit, as if telling herself it was none of her concern.

"You two have a good evening, then," she said.

That seemed to be their signal to leave. Seth and Devynn both thanked her—and the taciturn driver—for the ride, and they got out of the car and paused on the sidewalk. The street lamps were decorated with pine boughs that he knew members of the clan must have gathered up on Mingus Mountain, and big red velvet ribbons made them all the more festive. Farther down the street, closer to the English Kitchen, some people were moving about, but at this end of town, all the shops were closed, and no one had any reason for being here.

"Well, that helped," Devynn said. She put her gloved hands on her hips and glanced around. Although the evening air was still chilly, it felt a little warmer down here, as if being surrounded by buildings helped to shelter them from the worst of the cold. "And we must be pretty close to Christmas, since she made that comment about last-minute shopping."

Seth had thought much the same thing. "Sounds like it," he said, and then tugged at his overcoat. Now that the moment had come—now that they were about to cross the street and go into the apartment where he'd spent his entire life until he'd bought the bungalow—he found himself curiously awkward. There was so much to say, and he had no idea where to begin.

Seeming to sense some of his uneasiness, Devynn came closer and looped her arm through his. "It's going to be fine," she said. "You know your parents are going to be thrilled to see you."

He supposed so. No, it was his brother Charles who was the real question mark. But was he even still living in the apartment anymore? He and Abigail had bonded as consorts way back in June, after all, and Seth somehow doubted the *prima*-in-waiting would have wanted to wait very long to be joined to her fiancé in wedded bliss.

Not that there had been much bliss in that joining, if what he and Devynn had seen when they visited 1947 had been any indication.

"I hope so," he said briefly.

Arm in arm, they walked across the street and went around the back of the building. The old Dodge pickup truck the family used for mercantile business was parked back there, and Seth's throat tightened.

The last time he'd driven that truck, it had been to go on that doomed bootlegging expedition up to the mine shaft…with Devynn riding along in the bed, unbeknownst to him.

That trip hadn't turned out very well, and he knew it was only because of the intervention of the Wilcox healer in 1884 that the woman he loved more than life itself hadn't perished that day.

It had always been a fifty-fifty proposition as to whether the back door would be locked or not. Today it was, but a locked door was no impediment to one of witch-kind. Seth laid his hand on the knob, and it swung inward easily. As usual, the overhead light in the small, cramped foyer off the stockroom was on, and he had to be glad of that. His parents only turned it off when they had to change out the bulb, since they never knew when they might need to go down to the store to check on something.

The light it cast was enough to get them up the first flight of stairs, the ones that led to the main floor of the apartment. It occupied the second and third stories of the building, with the bedrooms at the very top. Seth found himself hoping he and Devynn wouldn't have to stay there, that his bungalow would still be empty at this point. He knew his cousin Margie had eventually moved into the house after it became clear he wasn't coming back, but he didn't know exactly when that had happened.

Now hand in hand, Seth and Devynn paused on the landing outside the apartment door. From inside, he heard the murmur of voices and a faint drift of music that he guessed was coming from the big radio in the living room, his father's pride and joy.

For some reason, hearing it made Seth feel a little less nervous. It was perfectly normal for them to be having dinner around this hour—his parents had always eaten early at this time of year —and even though he'd been gone for months, the realization that they'd kept up their regular routines reassured him.

Still, he had to take a second or two to gather himself before he raised his hand to knock.

The conversation paused, and then he heard footsteps moving toward the door. No doubt they were wondering who would be visiting at this hour, especially with the building locked up for the evening. True, members of the clan could come and go as they pleased, since locks were no real impediment, but still, barging in unannounced like that was considered quite rude.

And then the door opened, and his father stared out at him in astonishment. He didn't seem to have aged much during the time Seth had been gone, except to possibly have a few more threads of silver in his light brown hair.

That was good. Seth couldn't help thinking about how much his brother Charles had aged from 1926 to 1947, but of course, that had been a much longer span of time.

"Seth?"

"Hello, Father," Seth replied, knowing the words sounded horribly formal. But after spending months in the twenty-first century, he thought it better to compensate in the other direction rather than being as casual as most of the people he'd met in that future time.

No words beyond that, because his father immediately gathered him into a bear hug, holding onto him so tightly that Seth had to struggle to pull in a breath. When he let go, his gaze moved toward Devynn, who'd stood off to one side, a hopeful and yet also nervous expression on her lovely features.

"And Miss Rowe," Henry McAllister said. "It's very good to see you as well. Come inside."

There had been just the slightest edge under those words, a tone that told Seth his father wasn't as pleased to see Devynn as he'd just said. Well, that wasn't too surprising, not when he guessed his father probably saw her as the chief reason for his son's mysterious disappearance.

But at least he hadn't forbidden them from coming in.

They stepped inside, and immediately Seth heard his mother's voice coming from the dining room.

"Henry? Who was that at the door?"

"You'd better come see for yourself, Molly," his father replied.

The sound of a chair scraping against the floor was followed by quick footsteps, and then his mother appeared in the entry to the living room. She was wearing her favorite winter dress, the dark blue wool crepe one with the white collar, and her soft brown hair was pinned up in its usual low bun at the back of her neck. But when she saw Seth standing there just inside the door, her hand went to her throat.

"Oh, my dear Goddess," she whispered, and then she was rushing toward him, tears already glistening in the same blue eyes she shared with her son. "Seth!"

Her embrace was even more crushing than his father's had been, and Seth found himself blinking back tears of his own while his mother held him as if she planned to never let him go. When she finally pulled away, her hands went to his face, touching his cheeks as if she needed to reassure herself that he was real.

"We thought—" she began, then stopped and shook her head. "We didn't know what to think. You just vanished, and there was blood in the mine shaft, and we were so afraid…."

"I know, Mother. I'm sorry we worried you so much." Seth took her hands in his. "But we've been traveling, and we're back for Christmas."

Next to him, Devynn shifted slightly, as

though she wasn't completely thrilled with his choice of words.

But it was true. They had been traveling…just in time rather than space.

"Traveling?" Henry's straight brown brows—so like Seth's own—drew together. "Seth, you disappeared in June. It's been six months."

"I know it's been a long time," Seth said carefully. At some point, he would decide to tell them exactly what had happened, or whether it would be better to be somewhat vague about exactly where they were living. Whatever approach he used in the end, he'd already decided it would probably be better to come around to it slowly rather than revealing everything all at once. "But we're here now, and we're safe. That's what matters."

Molly's gaze had shifted to Devynn, who was standing quietly right inside the door, clearly trying not to intrude on the family reunion. "Miss Rowe," she said, then wiped her eyes with the back of her hand. "I'm so glad you're both all right. When you disappeared, no one knew what to think."

"Actually, Mother," Seth said quietly, "Deborah—Devynn," he added, realizing that they'd only known her by the much more common name she'd borrowed while in the past, "is my fiancée now."

The words hung in the air for a moment. Devynn stood there quietly, but Seth could tell she was doing her best to act reserved and polite, like a proper young woman of his era, and not say anything that might raise even more questions.

"Devynn?" Molly repeated, as though trying to get used to the unusual name. Then she went on, her voice rising slightly, "Your fiancée?"

"Yes," Seth said as he went to put his arm around Devynn's waist. She moved a little closer to him, and he could tell she was glad of the public display of affection, the clear intention to show his parents that they should now be regarded as a couple. "We've been through a lot together… and we discovered that we couldn't live without each other."

Devynn managed a smile, although Seth could feel how tense her slender body was. Not for the first time, he thought of her courage— not merely to volunteer to bring them back in time despite the risks associated with such a journey, but also to face his parents and confront them with the shocking revelation that the two of them were now engaged. "I hope you don't mind the surprise, Mrs. McAllister." She paused there, and although Seth couldn't sense anything different in the room, both his parents audibly gasped.

Her mother's bright blue eyes widened in

astonishment. "You're...you're a *witch?*" Molly said.

"I am," Devynn said calmly. "My gift is being able to conceal my witch nature, but obviously, there's no need to hide it from you now."

His father appeared to gather himself. "And which clan are you from? You can't be a McAllister."

However, something in his tone was doubtful. Not for the first time, Seth couldn't help being glad that Devynn didn't look very much like a Wilcox, a clan that tended to be quite dark, and resembled her father far more closely, with her blue-gray eyes and mid-brown hair.

"I'm not," she said simply. "I'm from the Winfield clan in Connecticut."

Well, that was half-true, anyway.

"You're a long way from home," Molly remarked, and Devynn nodded.

"Yes. But I had business here in Arizona."

She stopped there—as she must, since she was taking her cues from Seth and had obviously understood that he didn't want to broach the subject of time travel quite yet.

"I know this must all be quite overwhelming," she added.

"'Overwhelming,'" Molly echoed, and then a wavery smile tugged at her lips. "Oh, my dear, of course I don't mind that you felt the need to keep a few secrets. If Seth loves you, then you're family." She stepped forward and pulled Devynn into a warm embrace. "Welcome home."

The kindness in those words seemed to affect Devynn more than she'd probably thought they would. Her eyes closed briefly, and he could see the slight tension in her shoulders, a tightening that told him she was struggling to hold back tears of her own.

"Thank you," she murmured against Molly's shoulder. "That means everything to me."

Now looking brisk, Henry said, "Have you eaten? There's still plenty for everyone."

"Just stew," Seth's mother broke in, looking a little embarrassed to be offering something so plebeian to company. "But we wanted something simple since we'll be having our big dinner tomorrow night on Christmas Eve."

Relief surged through him. Yes, he and Devynn had already guessed that it was close to Christmas, but now it seemed as if she'd timed their arrival almost perfectly. Yes, they'd hoped to arrive on Christmas Eve day, but maybe this was even better, since it would give his parents a little extra time to come to terms with their unexpected appearance before the holiday arrived.

"Stew sounds wonderful," Seth said. "I know we're both hungry."

"Then come sit down," Molly urged them as

she led everyone into the dining room. "I'll just fetch some more table settings. Henry, could you get a few more napkins from the sideboard?"

In short order, Seth and Devynn had been seated at the dining room table, bowls full of his mother's delicious stew set in front of them. Devynn looked far more relaxed now that she had food to concentrate on—and was probably just as relieved as he that they'd gotten here pretty much when they needed to.

That didn't mean they didn't need to settle a few more things.

"How is my house?" Seth asked after he'd taken a few bites of stew and washed them down with some water. He wished it could have been wine, but the America of this time was still deep in Prohibition, and he knew his parents would never serve alcohol at their table. "I was hoping Devynn and I could stay there."

His mother's brows lifted slightly, and he guessed she was thinking such an arrangement didn't sound very proper. He and Devynn might have been engaged, but in 1926, that was still a far cry from being married.

"It's fine," his father said, and he also looked somewhat troubled. "Your cousin Margie has been asking how long we planned to leave it sitting empty like that, but we just told her we weren't going to make any big decisions until after the first of the year."

Well, that was a piece of good news. As for his parents' reservations about Devynn staying there unchaperoned....

"Devynn will stay in the guest room," Seth said. "It might look odd to some people, but I don't see the point in having her go to a hotel when I have the space right here."

His parents exchanged a glance. To some people, it might have looked inscrutable. Seth, on the other hand, knew they were only determining which of them should be the one to start throwing up some roadblocks.

Apparently, that task fell to his mother first, because she said, "Devynn could always go and stay with your Aunt Ruth again. I'm sure she'd love to have a guest for the holidays."

At once, Devynn sent him an alarmed look. While Seth knew Aunt Ruth had taken very good care of Devynn, he had no intention of allowing himself to be separated from the woman he loved. He'd gotten used to the much more relaxed customs and attitudes of the twenty-first century, and no way in the world was he going to backtrack.

"I'm sure she would," he said smoothly. "But Devynn and I want to be together, and if anyone has a problem with her staying in the guest room, then they can come and talk to me about it."

Henry set down his fork. "We're only trying to help—"

"I know you are," Devynn cut in. However, she kept her tone sweet, and it didn't look as if his father had taken any offense at the interruption. "And we appreciate it. But now that we're engaged, we really can't imagine being apart even for a few hours every night. It will be fine."

For a moment, his parents were silent, and Seth could tell they were trying to decide whether to push the matter any further or give it up as a lost cause.

Apparently, it was the latter, because then Molly said briskly, "But we'll need to send some fresh linens over with you, along with anything you might need to restock the kitchen. The pantry is bare now, of course, and anything in the linen closet will be stale from having been stored all these months."

"That's very kind of you," Devynn said. "Thank you."

His mother's eyes were suspiciously bright again. "It's no matter at all," she said. "Remember, you're family now."

Well, she seemed to be in his parents' eyes.

Now they'd just have to see how Charles viewed the matter....

3

As relieved as I was that Seth's parents had apparently decided to accept me as one of their own, I was still extremely happy to go home to our bungalow, where we could be alone. A wave of cognitive dissonance hit me as we stepped inside and I saw the place in its original form, just because I knew what it was like with a modern kitchen and bathroom, even though the original charm of the home had been preserved as much as possible. All the same, it still felt so very good to know that here we wouldn't have to watch every single thing we said.

For a few minutes, we busied ourselves with putting things away in the pantry and the cupboards, and putting fresh sheets on both beds. Obviously, Seth and I would share the one in the larger of the two bedrooms, but just in case Molly or anyone else came snooping, it seemed wise to make it look as if I was sleeping in the other one during my time here in Jerome.

Once all those tasks were handled, however, I said, "How much are you going to tell them?"

He'd just slipped off his jacket and turned to face me in his shirtsleeves. We'd also gotten a fire going in the hearth, and some of the chill in the room had already begun to dissipate, although I knew it would never get as warm as it did with modern central heat installed.

"I'm not sure yet," he said. "Either way, I want to wait until the time is right. I don't want to pile too many shocks on them all at once."

I supposed that was probably the smart way to handle the situation. Judging by a few of the things Molly had said at dinner, it seemed clear to me that she expected the two of us to get married soon and set up house here at the bungalow.

While both those wishes were technically fine, they were going to come true more than a hundred years from now, not in 1926.

"Okay," I said. "I just want to know that you'll give them some kind of closure before we leave."

"I will. Don't worry." He came to me then and pulled me into his arms, and bent down to press his lips against mine.

Yes, that was much better. My blood warmed, and right then, I wanted nothing more than to head into the bedroom and do all the things his parents had been worried about.

"Let's go to bed," I whispered, and Seth nodded.

"A wonderful idea."

Getting out of our 1920s clothes was a lot easier than the stuff we'd had to wear in the 1880s, when I'd been buried in so many layers, my elaborate bustle dresses had sometimes felt like portable prisons. Now, though, Seth and I were naked soon enough, snuggling under the covers…and finding all sorts of new ways to get warm.

Well, what his parents didn't know wouldn't hurt them.

During the meal at Henry and Molly's apartment, we'd learned that Charles would be coming over for dinner on Christmas Eve…and that he'd be bringing Abigail with him. I was less than enchanted by that prospect, mostly because I'd seen the kind of woman she'd turned out to be and didn't like her very much. Possibly, I should have been more charitable, since she'd fought chronic illnesses all her life and probably hadn't felt entirely well in a great many years. Then again, I'd known a few people who battled health issues like that in my own time and still weren't crotchety wrecks.

However, I told myself I'd put on my game face for Seth's sake, mostly because I understood that he had some things he needed to discuss with Charles. Not everything, of course—I knew Seth would never reveal what we'd learned during our time in 1947, about Abigail's continuing sickliness and their unhappy marriage—but even so, the two brothers needed to come to some kind of understanding. By nature, Seth was a forgiving person, and yet it was still hard for him to deal with the unpleasant reality of the way his brother had roped him into his bootlegging schemes.

Especially since that whole mess had ended with me getting shot in the stomach.

But at least Christmas morning sounded as though it would just be Seth's parents and the two of us, although Molly and Henry were expected at a big holiday dinner that night at the *prima's* house. By that point, I knew Seth and I would want to be on our way back to the twenty-first century, so at least I wouldn't have to deal with Abigail and Charles two nights in a row.

Molly had also informed us that the store would be closing early, at three-thirty, and that they'd love for us to come over and decorate the tree. I'd noticed the night before that a Christmas tree didn't seem to be anywhere in evidence—not that the McAllister apartment was really big enough for a person to hide something like that—and Seth had told me it was his family tradition to put it up on Christmas Eve and then keep it up through New Year's. It seemed strange not to have a tree around while all the other pre-holiday festivities were happening, but I knew every family did things a little differently, so I only nodded and told him that decorating the tree sounded like fun.

I didn't know for sure whether Seth's parents planned to tell everyone of our arrival, or whether they intended to keep things to themselves until they knew a little more about our intentions. With any luck, it would be the latter; I wasn't exactly looking forward to handing out the same lie after lie. If we lay low for most of the day and went over to Molly and Henry's apartment right at the appointed time, then I supposed it was possible that no one else in the clan would even know we were here in Jerome.

That morning had dawned crisp and clear, with frost painting delicate patterns on the windows of the bungalow. I'd awoken to find Seth already dressed, standing at the window in the living room and looking out at the quiet street beyond the postage-stamp front yard, wearing an expression I couldn't quite read.

"Second thoughts?" I asked as I slipped my arms around his waist.

He leaned back against me. "No. Just...it's strange, being back here. Everything looks exactly the way I remember it, but knowing what I know now about the future, about what happens to everyone...." The words trailed off there, and he shook his head. "I keep expecting to see changes that haven't happened yet."

I thought I understood what he meant. It was disconcerting to walk through a world that existed in a completely different context from the one we'd left behind. Here, his parents were still alive and healthy. Charles and Abigail weren't married yet, although Molly had told us the big day was set for early in January, the week after New Year's. And the mines were still operational, the town bustling with a prosperity we knew would come to an end in the next few decades.

But even though we might have been able to move through time, we couldn't do anything about the course it would take.

Seth and I made our way over to the mercantile around three-thirty. We'd decided that hanging out in the bungalow was probably the safest bet... not that we minded whiling away the hours with some more indoor activities...and we found Molly already bustling around her home, preparing for the evening's festivities. The apartment felt smaller than I remembered from our brief visit the night before, but it was warm and inviting, filled with scents of cinnamon and nutmeg.

"Oh, wonderful, you're here!" she said, and wiped her flour-dusted hands on her apron. Her face was bright with an energy I hadn't seen the previous evening—the kind of happiness that I knew must have come from the surprise of having the whole family together for the holidays. "Devynn, would you mind helping me with the bread? I always make an extra loaf for Christmas Eve, but I need to get started on the roast."

"Of course," I said, even as I inwardly prayed I'd be up to the task. A domestic goddess I was not, but I hoped having Molly right there to offer advice would save me from any massive blunders. "I'd love to help."

As we worked side by side in the cramped kitchen, she shared stories about Seth's childhood that had me laughing despite my underlying worry about our precarious situation. There was the time when he was ten and had tried to use his newly manifested translocation gift to reach the cookie jar on the top shelf, only to materialize halfway inside the pantry wall, his legs dangling comically while Henry had to carefully extract him.

"He was stuck there for twenty minutes," Molly said. Her eyes twinkled at the memory, although I had a feeling she probably hadn't been quite as cheerful back when it had happened. "Henry was so worried about hurting him that he dismantled half the pantry shelf by shelf. And Seth just kept saying, 'I can get out myself, Dad!' and trying to blink away, which only made things worse."

After that, she told me about an incident when Seth was twelve and Charles had convinced his little brother to help him "reorganize" the mercantile's inventory by moving everything to the opposite side of the shop. It seemed the reasoning had been that doing so would make the store look more interesting, but it had created utter chaos when customers couldn't find the items they needed, and Henry had to take time out from an already busy schedule to put everything back in its proper place.

"Charles was always the instigator," Molly said with a smile. "But Seth was also willing to go along with his schemes. He idolized his big brother, you know. He would have followed him anywhere." Her expression sobered, and she paused, a pepper mill idle in one hand. "I think that's partly why what happened between them this summer hurt him so badly."

I concentrated on kneading the bread dough and did my best to keep my expression neutral. "They'll work it out," I said, even as I hoped I wasn't being overly optimistic. Something about Charles McAllister had always set my teeth on edge.

Molly picked up the roast, now properly seasoned, and set it in a big cast-iron pan. "I hope so. Seth's always been so determined—even as a little boy, if he set his mind to something, there was no stopping him. But he doesn't hold grudges, not really. He just needs time to process things."

Yes, that sounded just like Seth, so I nodded...even as I wondered if this was the one time when he actually would find it difficult to forgive.

The rest of the afternoon was pleasant enough, though, with more cheerful anecdotes and preparations for the evening meal. Molly showed me the family's collection of Christmas ornaments, each one with its own story. There was the delicate glass star that had belonged to Seth's grandmother, the wooden angels that Henry had carved during his and Molly's first Christmas as a married couple, and the slightly lopsided clay ornaments that Seth and Charles had made as children.

"Seth was so proud of this one," Molly said, holding up a lumpy clay reindeer that was missing one antler. "He was six, and he worked on it for hours. When it came out of the kiln at the school-house, he ran all the way home to show it to us."

As she spoke, I found myself studying her face, trying to memorize every detail. I'd met Molly McAllister in the past, of course, but we hadn't spent enough time together for me to truly know her as a real person. Now I could see where Seth got his determination, his friendliness, and his love of family. Molly was slight and slender, a few inches shorter than I, and didn't seem like someone who could have borne two such tall sons, but she had a spine of iron.

As five o'clock approached, however, my stomach began to knot with apprehension. I'd been dreading this reunion between the brothers ever since we'd decided to make this trip. Seth had told me some of what had transpired between him and Charles before that near-fatal encounter at the mine shaft—the bootlegging, the pressure to take over more responsibilities than Seth should have had to shoulder on his own.

The way Charles had used family loyalty to manipulate him into taking risks he otherwise never would have even contemplated.

And I couldn't forget how Charles's actions had led directly to me being shot, to the desperate time jump that had changed both our lives forever. Seth might have forgiven his brother, but I wasn't sure I had. Every time I thought about that moment as Lionel Allenby's bullet lodged in my gut...the pain and terror and the certainty that I was going to die...a burst of rage would flash through me all over again.

Still, I knew I needed to put all that aside if I was going to get through tonight.

Charles arrived right on time, with Abigail on his arm. She looked pretty much the same as she had the time I'd encountered her right before her twenty-first birthday, with pale blonde hair knotted low on her neck, although today she wore a dress of soft blue wool that somehow managed to make her seem even more fragile, rather than the lacy white summer frock she'd had on during our first meeting. Her pale eyes seemed to survey her surroundings with a kind of distant regard, as if her thoughts were somewhere else entirely.

"Seth," Charles said, his voice too neutral. "Mom told me you were back."

The two brothers stood facing each other in the living room, and I could practically see the tension crackling between them, sharp and hot as the sparks flying in the hearth.

"Hello, Charles," Seth replied evenly. "I'd like you to meet my fiancée, Devynn Rowe."

At those words, Abigail's pale eyes widened dramatically, and her gaze darted between Seth and me with something that looked almost like envy. I remembered then how he had been her first choice, how she'd wanted him to be her consort, even though the universe clearly had different plans.

Hopefully, she wasn't still carrying any kind of a torch for him, or this evening might turn out to be even more awkward than I'd feared.

Charles's mouth actually fell open for a moment before he managed to recover his composure.

"Miss Rowe," he said, his tone stiff. "A pleasure."

"Likewise," I replied, although we both knew that wasn't entirely true.

Molly, bless her, jumped into the silence before it could get too awkward. "It's a wonderful surprise, isn't it? Our Seth, engaged! And at Christmastime, no less. Come, everyone—let's sit down to dinner."

We all headed into the dining room, which felt even smaller with all of us crowded around the table. Although I did what I could to concentrate on the wonderful food, the undercurrents of tension at the table made every bite difficult to swallow. Nothing Charles said could exactly be called hostile, and yet something in his tone and the sideways, almost irritated glances he sent in his brother's direction told me he was less than thrilled that we were there. Seth did his best to ignore the little jabs and instead complimented his mother on the food, but I could tell from his ever-tightening jaw muscles that he wasn't happy, either.

To be honest, I didn't even know what Charles's game was. He'd been there at the mine—he'd seen me get shot and the two of us disappear. Sure, he'd probably been a little stumped about what had actually happened, just because in general, Seth's gift wasn't strong enough to tele-port two people at once, but maybe he'd thought in that moment of extremity, his brother's translo-cation talent had strengthened enough to send us both somewhere else.

And also, Charles hadn't known about my ability to travel in time.

"So...I'm curious how you could disappear someplace where there weren't any phones or even telegraphs," Charles said as he cut his roast beef with unnecessary force. "It would have been nice to know whether you were alive or dead."

"Charles," Henry said, his tone quiet but full of warning nonetheless.

"No, Dad, I think it's a fair point," Charles

continued, and didn't even look at his father. "The least you can do is let your family know you're all right. Don't you think so, Miss Rowe?"

Seth tensed beside me, and under the table, I laid a quelling hand on his knee. "I think," I said carefully, "that sometimes circumstances are more complicated than they appear from the outside."

"'Complicated.'" Charles chuckled, but there was no humor in the sound. "That's one word for it."

Abigail had remained largely silent throughout the meal, picking at her food with birdlike delicacy. But now she spoke up, her voice soft but carrying clearly across the tense silence at the table. "I'm sure Seth had his reasons for leaving," she said. "Although it does seem rather sudden, this engagement. I'm sure I had no idea you'd formed any kind of attachment while Miss Rowe was in town."

Seth's eyes narrowed. "That's because we didn't believe it was anyone else's business."

Molly made a warning sound, and he pulled in a breath and picked up his knife and fork so he could cut another piece of roast beef.

Apparently, Abigail didn't seem to notice the exchange between mother and son, because she went on, "It's just that when someone disappears for months and then returns engaged to a woman he barely knows...." She gave a delicate shrug. "Well, it raises questions, don't you think?"

I suppose it did. However, I knew Seth was still deciding what kind of answers he could give...and also knew he had no intention of uttering them anywhere near Abigail McAllister.

Henry and Molly tried valiantly to keep the conversation on neutral topics—the weather, the Christmas decorations around town, plans for the New Year, and Charles and Abigail's upcoming nuptials—but the undercurrent of tension at the table was impossible to ignore. I found myself watching Charles carefully, trying to reconcile this fiery man with the bitter, careworn person we'd encountered in 1947. That Charles had been worn down by decades of an unhappy marriage and the weight of believing he'd caused his brother's death. This Charles was much more volatile, and I wasn't sure what to expect from him.

Finally, Seth pushed his chair back from the table with a loud scrape. "Charles, I think you and I need to talk. Outside."

His brother set down the fork he'd been holding. "I don't think that's necessary—"

"Yes, I think that's a discussion you can leave until a later time," Molly cut in. "It's Christmas Eve!"

Seth's expression softened. "I'm sorry, Mom,

but I know Charles and I need to do this." His tone was firm enough that it appeared Molly realized there was no point in arguing with him. Then he turned to me, and I could see the determination in his clear blue eyes. "Devynn, would you come with us? We don't have any secrets from each other."

Charles's face suffused with anger—right then, I was glad this had been a dry dinner, thanks to Prohibition, since I didn't want to think what he would have been like if he'd actually been drinking—and Abigail's mouth pursed with what might have been disapproval. But neither of them protested, so the three of us excused ourselves and stepped out onto the landing, and Seth closed the door behind us.

"All right," Charles said as he crossed his arms. "Let's have it, then. Where the hell have you been for the past six months? And don't give me any more nonsense about 'traveling.' I'm not an idiot, Seth. I saw you and Devynn disappear after Allenby shot her. Where did you go?"

Seth was quiet for a long moment, his hands shoved into the pockets of his wool trousers. When he finally spoke, his voice was gentler than I'd expected. "As Devynn said, that's…complicated. But first, I think you might have some things you should say to me."

Charles's composure cracked then, and I saw a flash of the guilt he'd been carrying written plainly in his features. His shoulders sagged, and he suddenly looked much older than his years, reminding me of the version of himself we'd met in 1947.

"Seth, I'm sorry," he said. The words came out quickly, as if he somehow knew if he didn't say them all at once, he'd never say them at all. "It was my fault. Dragging you into the bootlegging ring, and then what happened to you, Devynn—I never meant for any of it to go so wrong."

Expression almost stricken, Seth replied in a near-murmur, "I know you didn't."

"When you disappeared like that and never came back," Charles continued, his words coming even faster now, as if a dam had burst, "I thought —I thought I'd gotten you killed. Both of you. And for what? A chance to win back Mary Towne? Some stupid idea that I could impress her family with a big house and a fat bankroll?" He turned to me then, and for a second, his mouth tightened. Somehow I knew he was forcing himself to address me directly, and I knew then that our dislike was mutual. "Devynn, I should never have involved Seth in any of it. I should never have put you in danger. When Allenby shot you...."

My throat tightened. I'd heard about the aftermath of that night only in 1947, when we'd learned that Lionel Allenby had supposedly died in an "accident" shortly after shooting me. I'd never really considered what Charles must have gone through in those immediate moments, watching us both disappear and not knowing if I'd died in his brother's arms.

"It's all right," I said quietly. "We're both fine."

"But where were you?" The anguish in Charles's voice was painful to hear. "My mother's been putting on a brave face, but I know she's been heartbroken at the way Seth disappeared. Dad's aged ten years. I did that. I caused all of it because I was too proud to accept that Mary Towne was never going to come back to me."

Seth stepped closer to his brother. "Charles, it's all right. Devynn and I are fine. And what happened wasn't entirely your fault."

Hands now shoved in his pockets, Charles retorted, "How can you say that? If I hadn't been running moonshine—"

"If Lionel Allenby hadn't been a greedy, violent man who saw Devynn as a threat to his operation," Seth broke in, voice firm enough that his brother seemed to subside for the moment. "If I had been honest with you about how I felt about the whole business instead of just going along with it. If I had told Devynn the truth from the beginning instead of trying to hide what I was doing. There were a lot of factors that led to that night, Charles. You weren't the only one who made mistakes."

Charles stared at his brother for a long moment, clearly wrestling with himself. "But I was the one who got you involved in the first place. I knew you'd do anything for family, and I exploited that."

"Yes, you did," Seth agreed, although his voice was quiet, almost contemplative, rather than angry. "And that hurt. It hurt more than the physical danger, if I'm being honest. I trusted you, and you manipulated me."

Charles flinched slightly, but that didn't stop him from responding. "I know. I've been living with that knowledge every day since you disappeared. I keep thinking about that last conversation we had, the way you looked at me when you realized what I was really asking of you...."

"But I forgive you," Seth said. "For all of it. I forgive you because you're my brother, and because I can see how much you regret it."

Charles's face finally crumpled then, and he pulled Seth into a fierce embrace. "I've missed you," he said, his voice rough with emotion. "And I thought I'd never get the chance to tell you how sorry I was."

When they finally separated, their eyes shone

with unshed tears. Charles turned to me with something approaching a genuine smile for the first time all evening.

"And congratulations on your engagement," he said. "I can see why Seth fell for you—you've got grit, and it's obvious you've stood by him through whatever adventure the two of you have been on. He's lucky to have found someone who won't run at the first sign of trouble."

I managed a smile in return, although even now some part of me couldn't help wondering if all this was genuine, or whether Seth's brother had made a show of an apology simply to please their parents and keep the peace at Christmas. However, I kept those concerns to myself as I said, "Thank you, Charles. That means a lot."

"Have you set a date?" he asked, and I could see him making an effort to be the supportive brother-in-law. "Abigail and I are getting married in just a few weeks. She wanted the wedding to happen before she turns twenty-two, and her birthday is on the fifteenth of January."

Seth and I exchanged glances. No way in the world could we say we were getting married in only a week...a hundred and twenty years from now.

"We're still discussing the details," he said diplomatically, and to my relief, his brother didn't press him for any further information.

As we made our way back inside the apartment, I thought the atmosphere now felt noticeably lighter. Charles actually joked with Seth about the amount of roast beef he'd eaten at dinner, and even Abigail seemed to have thawed slightly, asking me polite questions about my background and interests.

But I found myself growing increasingly anxious as the evening wore on. I excused myself to the small bathroom down the hall, claiming I needed to freshen up. But really, I needed a moment alone to test something that had been worrying me all day.

I closed my eyes and concentrated, trying to make the smallest possible jump forward in time, just a few seconds, enough to know my gift was still working properly. I reached for that strange sensation of temporal displacement, that odd little blink that told me I'd gone somewhen else.

And…nothing.

Cold flooded my veins, and I clutched the edges of the pedestal sink to steady myself. I tried again, pushing harder, focusing all my energy on that elusive feeling of sliding between one moment and the next. My pulse quickened as I felt absolutely nothing—no tingle of magic, no sense that I'd blinked a few moments into the future, nothing but the solid, immovable present.

My time travel gift, which had always been

unpredictable and difficult to control, now seemed to have disappeared entirely.

I pulled in a shaky breath, then wetted one edge of a towel and dabbed cold water on my face, taking care not to remove any of the careful cosmetics I'd applied before Seth and I left the bungalow earlier that afternoon. A glance in the mirror above the sink told me my skin was pale despite the rouge, my eyes wide with barely concealed fear. I forced myself to take several deep breaths, doing what I could to calm the racing of my heart. There had to be an explanation for what had just gone wrong. Maybe the emotional intensity of the day had affected me somehow, or maybe it was the stress of maintaining our cover story...or the simple fact that my gift had always been temperamental.

But as I rejoined the others, forcing myself to smile and help Molly clear the table, then cut slices of cherry pie for everyone, an uneasy sensation was growing in the pit of my stomach. If I couldn't access my abilities, how were we going to get home? And what would happen if we were trapped here permanently, in a time that wasn't ours, living a lie that would eventually catch up with us?

The thought of never seeing my own family again, of being forever cut off from the life I'd built in the twenty-first century, made my hands tremble as I reached for my coffee cup. Seth caught my eye across the table, his expression questioning, and I managed a small smile that I hoped was reassuring.

But inside, I was beginning to panic.

4

SETH COULD TELL SOMETHING WAS bothering Devynn after their Christmas Eve dinner at his parents' house, but since she didn't seem willing to volunteer any information, he decided to let it go. She could have merely been trying to process the events of the evening and Charles's apology, or she could have been worrying that they might not be able to make their escape before the fancy meal planned at the *prima's* house on the evening of Christmas Day. Over dinner, Abigail had insisted that they attend, and even though both he and Devynn had done their best to demur, she'd made it sound like a command performance.

Which meant the two of them needed to leave after Christmas morning breakfast at his parents' apartment was done and they would ostensibly have some of the day to themselves before they had to head over to Mabel's house.

At least Molly had said breakfast would be late, not until nine o'clock, so Seth knew he and Devynn wouldn't have to worry about getting up at the crack of dawn to make themselves presentable. They didn't have any presents to exchange that morning, not when their "real" Christmas would take place many decades from now, but he was just fine with a more physical way of showing their love for one another, luxuriating in one another's embrace until it was time to head into the bathroom and get ready.

Skies were bright and clear as they often were on Christmas in this part of the world, and the little snow that had remained from the storm a few days before they'd arrived now appeared to have mostly melted. Devynn put on the beautiful red dress she'd bought from the seller on Etsy, and although Seth wore the same suit, he'd freshened it up with a different shirt and tie.

Getting ready in the primitive bathroom only reminded him of how much such things had changed over the intervening decades. However, he told himself to consider the current setup as an adventure, sort of like roughing it at a campground out in the middle of the wilderness, rather than thinking of it as something he would have to endure on a regular basis.

All the same, navigating the balky plumbing and the ice-cold floors definitely helped him appreciate the twenty-first century that much more.

Once he and Devynn had decided on this trip back in time, they'd bought presents from an antique store down in Cottonwood—a fine watch chain for Henry; a pretty tortoiseshell comb for Abigail, who did have lovely hair despite her perpetual ill health; a silver-handled valet set for Charles; a gold locket for Molly. Seth had put a photo of himself inside the locket, thinking he could leave that image with his mother, even if he couldn't stay here in 1926. One of the McAllister cousins had run the image through Photoshop so it looked like something that might have been taken during the correct time period, and he hoped Molly would like it.

Finding period-appropriate wrapping paper for the gifts had been impossible, so Devynn had suggested that they wrap each gift in a vintage handkerchief, which they'd also found at the antique store. Possibly this was unconventional, but better the handkerchiefs than trying to explain where that crazy metallic wrapping paper had come from, or worse, the little paper gift bags she tended to favor because she'd frankly confessed as the holiday season began that she was terrible at wrapping presents.

They set out arm in arm, both protected from the chilly air by their overcoats. Despite the bright sun that shone down on them, it was still very cold outside, and Seth was looking forward to the fire he knew would be blazing at his parents' apartment.

The scent of cinnamon rolls seemed to drift down the stairwell long before they approached the front door, and his stomach rumbled. All he'd had so far this morning was a cup of coffee, and after his exertions with Devynn a few hours earlier, his body was telling him it needed a lot more fuel than that.

His mother opened the door almost as soon as he knocked. "Merry Christmas!" she exclaimed, and then hugged him and Devynn.

"Merry Christmas," they replied almost in unison, and sent a goofy grin at each other. Seth had been careful not to leave any marks on her neck during their lovemaking, but he still wondered if she looked a little too glowing and content for someone who supposedly had slept alone in a cold bed the night before.

Luckily, his mother didn't seem to notice anything out of the ordinary as she stepped out of the way so they could come inside. A fire blazed in the hearth, just as he'd hoped, and in the corner, the ornaments on the Christmas tree glittered in its reflected light. It wasn't quite as brilliant as the trees he'd seen in the twenty-first century, with their myriad of electric lights, but still, he thought it had its own quieter sort of beauty.

He didn't see Charles or Abigail, although his father had risen from his favorite chair to greet them, his hug almost as enthusiastic as Molly's. An inquiring glance at his mother, and her shoulders lifted ever so slightly.

"Charles sent word that Abigail was feeling a little tired this morning, so they decided to stay in and rest up for her mother's big Christmas dinner tonight." Although Molly's tone didn't shift all that much, Seth could tell his mother was disappointed by this development. However, she only continued, still smiling, "And since we had them with us last night, I suppose we can't begrudge Abigail the peace and quiet she needs."

"Then I suppose we'll leave our presents for them under the tree here," Seth replied, and Molly only tilted her head.

"No, you can just take them with you tonight, dear."

Next to him, Devynn shifted her weight slightly. He knew what she was thinking—that there was no chance in hell that they'd be at the *prima's* holiday dinner this evening.

However, he knew he couldn't voice that thought aloud, so he just nodded and said, "Of course. But I'll put them under there for now."

And hope he could conveniently forget them in the bustle of leaving.

Then Molly asked if they wanted tea or coffee, and they both said tea would be lovely. Once they'd been given their beverages, she returned to the kitchen so she could finish breakfast—namely, to scramble a big batch of brown eggs that Seth guessed she'd gotten from their cousin Emily, who had a large flock of chickens, along with frying enough bacon to feed a small army.

This was always how it had gone on Christmas morning—they would eat their fill, and then afterward, they would go and open their presents. Or rather, this was the schedule the family had followed once the two boys were old enough not to want to immediately open presents and see what Santa had left them. The McAllister clan might have followed the old ways and worshipped the goddess Brigid…but they'd also made sure their children believed in Santa for as long as possible.

And although Seth was a little sad for his parents that Charles wouldn't be there that morning, he was forced to admit that this gathering seemed much more cheery and relaxed with just the four of them. To his relief, his mother didn't seem inclined to probe too much into where he and Devynn had been these last six months, as though she knew she wouldn't get any real answers. No, she was much more interested in talking about what they planned to do next.

"You know everyone will want you to choose a date," she said, and sent a significant glance toward Devynn, as if she knew it was the bride's prerogative to make such an important decision.

Pink touched her cheeks, but she sounded even enough as she replied, "Probably sometime in the spring," she replied. "Winter weddings can be nice, but I want something with flowers that didn't come from a hothouse. So...maybe May?"

"It's absolutely beautiful around here at that time of year," his mother said, looking pleased. "Don't you think so, Henry?"

Seth's father had been in the middle of lifting a forkful of scrambled eggs to his mouth, so he waited until he was done chewing before he answered. "May's a good time. It's warm but not really hot yet."

With that settled—in Molly's mind, anyway—the conversation moved on to the all-important topic of the wedding dress. Once again, Devynn flushed a little during that conversation, but Seth hoped his mother would think that was due to maidenly modesty and not because Devynn simply didn't know all that much about bridal fashions of the 1920s.

And definitely not that the all-important dress had already been purchased and was hiding out at their friend Bellamy's house. Bellamy was Devynn's maid-of-honor and had declared that their bungalow was much too small for the gown to be successfully hidden for so many weeks, so it had been spirited away just as soon as the final alterations had been done. Seth still didn't know whether all this top-level secrecy was required, but he hadn't protested. If nothing else, it would be fun to be utterly surprised when Devynn appeared and walked down the admittedly short aisle set up in the lounge at The Asylum.

After they were done eating—and after he and Devynn had insisted on clearing the table—they went into the living room. The fire had died down a bit, so Henry gave it a few expert pokes before they took their various seats.

"Sorry about the wrapping paper...or lack thereof," Seth said as he picked up his parents' presents. "We didn't have time to go out and find some."

"It's fine," his mother assured him. "Wrapping paper is wasteful, while your father and I will be able to use these handkerchiefs for years."

That was the response he'd been hoping for. Smiling, he accepted the gift his mother handed him—and was surprised she had one for Devynn as well, a small box that she gave his fiancée with a smile.

When would she have even had time to buy something for her unexpected guest?

As soon as that thought went through his mind, he wanted to shake his head at himself. Right below them was the store his parents owned; it wasn't as if Molly couldn't have gone downstairs after dinner last night and found something she thought would work.

"Thank you," Devynn replied, also looking a little startled. "I really wasn't expecting you to get me anything."

"Nonsense," Molly said briskly. "You're going to marry our son. Of course we needed to get you a Christmas present."

A smile, and Devynn opened the box. Inside was an engraved silver compact, something he'd seen in the store months earlier but hadn't been sure if his parents would sell anytime soon. Most of the residents of Jerome—the McAllisters included—weren't big on frivolities.

"It's beautiful," she said.

"I'm glad you like it," Molly replied, then nodded at her husband. "Henry, open yours."

He unwrapped the linen handkerchief that had concealed the watch chain, and his eyes widened a little. Seth could understand why; the chain had been quite expensive in the twenty-first century, and although of course it would have cost much less in the 1920s, it was still something of an extravagant gift. However, money wasn't a problem for him and Devynn, and he'd wanted to get something he knew his father would never have bought for himself.

"This is...very generous," he said after a pause of a second or two. "Thank you, Seth—and you, too, Devynn."

"I'm glad you like it," Seth replied. Devynn was smiling...and possibly looked a little relieved as well, as if she hadn't been quite certain how their gift would be received.

"Your turn," Molly said, and although Seth wanted to protest, he knew she wouldn't hear of unwrapping her present until he'd opened his. That had been another tradition in their family—she always went last.

The box his mother had placed by his chair was quite large, and he wondered what could be in it.

Probably not a puppy, he thought with an inner grin. He and Devynn had discussed getting a dog, but they'd both decided it would be better to wait to add to their little family until the wedding was over and everything had settled down again.

No, when he unwrapped the present, he found a beautiful beaver-felt hat inside, a jaunty charcoal gray fedora that he knew must have also come from the mercantile.

"It's great, Mom," he said, and lifted it out and set it on his head. Of course, it fit perfectly; his mother knew his hat size as well as she knew her own.

Whether he'd have much need of it in the future was an entirely different matter, but he thought it would probably serve him well the next time he and Devynn went to a vintage dance event.

"Oh, good," she said, looking relieved, even though she must have known it would fit him without needing even a single session with a hat block and a steamer. "I thought that color would go very well with your eyes."

Yes, he'd always looked good in gray.

Smiling, he thanked her again, then returned the hat to its box. "Your turn, Mom."

She pulled away the handkerchief to reveal the small box inside. Devynn had found the vintage leather-wrapped jewelry box at the antique store, and even though the locket was something they'd purchased separately, they'd both agreed the two items went well together.

Molly removed the lid, and, just like her husband's, her eyes widened for a second. Then she lifted out the gold locket on its slender chain, and the small diamonds and rubies embedded in the engraved pattern twinkled in the firelight.

"It's beautiful," she breathed, although her

expression turned stern a moment later. "You really didn't need to buy me something so extravagant, Seth."

"Maybe not," he replied with an easy smile. "But I wanted to."

Very carefully, she opened the locket to look inside. For a moment, she was silent as she gazed down at the photo he'd placed there, and tears sparkled in her eyes.

"Thank you, Seth," she said, very quietly. One hand went to her throat, but then she seemed to gather herself as she turned toward her husband. "Henry, could you please put it on for me?"

At once, Seth's father took the locket from her. A moment passed as he fumbled with the delicate clasp, but then he had the chain placed around her neck and managed to fasten it.

"I think it suits you very well," Devynn said, and Molly smiled.

"Oh, I think it might be too fancy for a shopkeeper, but that doesn't mean I won't wear it proudly." Again, she looked over at Seth. "I know you don't want me to say you shouldn't have, so I won't. I'll only say thank you again."

Her voice trembled a little on the last word, and Seth got up from his chair so he could go over and give her a hug. Not for the first time, he thought of how small and fragile she felt when he wrapped his arms around her. A false impression, he knew. Underneath that delicate exterior, his mother was made of steel.

He hoped that strength would help her when he and Devynn disappeared…this time forever.

After they were finished with presents and did the dishes—Molly protested vociferously and said she could take care of them herself, but Seth and Devynn only told her that was part of her gift—the two of them took a walk around Jerome to work off some of the rich food and give his parents a little time to themselves. The December air was crisp but not unpleasant, and with the sun shining down on them, it was warm enough that Seth unbuttoned his overcoat.

"Your mother seemed to really love the locket," Devynn said as they made their way down the steep slope of Hull Street, past what was currently a garage but in the future would be Lawrence Memorial Hall, more commonly known as Spook Hall, the venue for Jerome's big Halloween dance and many other events.

"She did." Seth's throat was a little tight, and he cleared it before he added, "I'm glad we were able to find something she likes so much."

They walked in silence for a few more minutes, but Seth could sense something shifting in Devynn's mood. Her steps had slowed slightly, and when he glanced over at her, he could see the tense set of her shoulders beneath the heavy overcoat.

"What time is it?" she asked.

Seth pulled out his pocket watch—another prop they'd gotten as part of their 1926 disguises—and glanced down at it. "Almost noon."

"We should probably head on down to the bungalow, then." She paused before taking a breath. "I think it's time."

Breakfast flip-flopped in his gut. Even though he'd known this moment would come, now that it was here, he found himself wanting to postpone it just a little longer.

"Dinner at Mabel's isn't until five," he pointed out, although that argument sounded weak even to him.

Devynn's steps paused, and then she turned to face him. "If we wait too long, your parents are going to expect us to go with them to Mabel's house. And once we're there…."

She didn't need to finish the sentence. Seth knew that once they were at the *prima's* Christmas dinner, surrounded by family members, there would be no graceful way to leave. They'd be trapped, at least until late in the evening, and by then it would be that much harder to get away. His parents very likely would invite them to the apartment afterward, would want to spend more time with them, and his and Devynn's window for escape would only grow narrower.

In his mind, he knew that might be a silly way to look at the situation when they had all of time to play with…but he also understood that she had stretched her abilities by bringing them here, and if they didn't stick to their original plan, that might throw her off too much.

"I know," he said heavily. "You're right."

They walked the rest of the way to the bungalow in silence, both lost in their own thoughts. Once they were inside, Devynn sat down heavily on the sofa, and Seth could see how tired she truly was, a weariness betrayed by the faint shadows under her blue-gray eyes and the taut set of her full mouth. He thought she'd slept all right the night before, but he had to admit the mattress had felt thin and lumpy after the luxurious memory-foam one they enjoyed in the future.

"Are you sure you're up for this?" he asked as he settled himself beside her.

"I have to be." She leaned against him, and he wrapped his arm around her shoulders, wishing he could lend her some of his own magical strength so she wouldn't have to tax herself so much. "Besides, what choice do we have?"

None, really. They both knew that. While he was glad they'd come here—glad that he was able to get some closure, and at least let his parents know that he was well, and happy—he also understood that this wasn't his world anymore.

They needed to get back to the place where they both belonged.

Devynn reached over to take both his hands in hers. Not for the first time, Seth wondered what would happen if he let go.

He probably didn't want to know.

"Ready?" she asked, and he nodded.

"Ready."

The world dissolved around them, and he tightened his grip on her fingers. At least he knew that this moment of travel was really nothing more than a fraction of a second, less than a tenth of an eyeblink.

When they emerged from that millisecond of darkness, Seth immediately realized something was wrong. The light coming through the windows was different from what they'd left behind in the twenty-first century, gray and subdued. And when he looked outside, he could see snow falling steadily.

Because he liked to know what the weather

was doing, he'd checked the forecast before they left. It wasn't supposed to snow again until after Christmas.

"Damn," Devynn muttered beside him.

Seth got up and walked to the window, then peered through the cold glass, whose chill was readily apparent even from a few inches away. The snow was coming down in thick, heavy flakes, and several inches had already accumulated on the ground. This definitely wasn't the mild winter weather they'd been enjoying in their own time.

"When are we?" he asked, even though he was already dreading the answer.

Devynn rose from the sofa and walked over to the kitchen, where she'd apparently spied a newspaper lying on the table—a paper he knew hadn't been there when they'd left. "December 23rd, 1925."

A date when he would have been living here at the house. Thank the Goddess the bungalow was currently empty—he guessed that his former self would have been at work on that snowy Wednesday a year ago— but they sure weren't when they were supposed to be.

No, they were around a hundred and twenty years too early.

"It's all right," Seth said, trying to keep his voice calm. "At least no one was around to see us show up here. We just need to jump forward again."

But even as the words left his lips, he could see how pale Devynn had become, how her hands trembled slightly. Despite her claims about practicing, he knew that her gift was very difficult to control, and he wasn't sure how many jumps she could attempt before she wore herself out completely.

"I can do it," she said firmly, forestalling any questions.

Seth wasn't entirely convinced, but he knew better than to argue.

"Okay."

And he went over to where she stood so he could knot his fingers in hers once again.

This time, when the world blurred around them, he felt something go wrong even before they reemerged from that other-when between milliseconds. The transition was rougher, almost jarring, and when reality reasserted itself, he was nearly knocked off his feet by a wall of oppressive heat.

Sunlight blazed through the windows with an intensity that made him squint, and the air was thick and stifling. Even inside the bungalow, it felt like an oven.

"Oh, hell," Devynn muttered.

Seth looked around the bungalow for another

newspaper, but he didn't need one to know they'd overshot their mark. The brutal heat, the angle of the sun, the way the light fell across the familiar furniture—this was summer. Deep summer, from the feel of it.

"July 1927," he said after a quick glance into the kitchen, where a calendar had always hung. Other details about the bungalow felt wrong, though, like the curtains at the windows and the pillows on the sofa, and it hit him.

That would have been a year after he disappeared. By then, his cousin Margie would have already moved into the little house. It didn't look as if she'd replaced the furniture—probably because she couldn't afford it—but she'd apparently changed whatever small details she could.

"Well, crap," Devynn said, her voice weaker than ever. She swayed slightly on her feet, and Seth quickly moved to steady her.

"That's enough," he said, making sure he sounded firm enough that she wouldn't argue with him. "You need to give yourself a chance to rest."

Where, he had no idea. Sure, his cousin didn't appear to be home at the moment, but she could come back at any time. And if she found the two of them there....

Well, that would require a lot more explanations than he currently had the energy for.

"No." Devynn shook her head, although she

put a hand up to her temple, as if even that simple movement had hurt. "I can do one more. We have to get out of here."

Seth wanted to argue, but he could see the determination in her eyes. And more than that, he could see the fear. They were trapped in the wrong time, and she feared she might not be able to take them to the correct one.

"All right," he said reluctantly. "But if the next jump doesn't work, we'll have to find a place where we can wait this out. You need time to recover."

She nodded, though he wasn't sure she was really listening. All her attention appeared to be focused inward, gathering what remained of her strength.

The world dissolved around them, and Seth could almost feel Devynn's gift falter halfway through the transition, sense the way reality seemed to stutter and skip around them like a broken phonograph record. For a terrifying moment, he thought they might be lost completely, trapped between moments in some gray limbo.

Then they crashed back into the world with enough force to send them both stumbling.

At least the light seemed right this time—the bright afternoon sun of the Christmas Day they'd left behind. But Devynn collapsed onto the sofa, her face ashen and her breathing shallow.

Oh, hell. Seth sat down next to her, wondering what he should do. Call the healer, probably, but he really didn't feel up to explaining to Helen exactly what was wrong with Devynn.

"I'm okay," she said. The words came out in a breathy gasp, contradicting that claim. "Just...give me a minute."

Seth reached over and touched her forehead with the back of his hand. The skin was fever-hot despite the cool air in the bungalow.

"This is insane," he said. "You can't keep doing this to yourself."

"Like we have a choice?" Her voice was hoarse, barely more than a whisper. "If we don't leave soon—"

She was right, and they both knew it. But seeing her like this, so obviously depleted and struggling, Seth could feel his resolve waver. Was getting back to the twenty-first century really worth risking her health? Her life?

Before he could voice those thoughts, Devynn struggled to sit up.

"What time is it?" she asked.

Seth checked his watch again. "Two-thirty."

Two and a half hours until they were expected at the *prima's* house. Two and a half hours to make their final preparations and say goodbye to a life he'd already abandoned once.

This time, though, he would try to leave some kind of words behind, something to let everyone know this was something he'd chosen.

"We need to go soon," Devynn said. "Before your parents come looking for us."

Seth nodded. His chest was tight; he might have understood deep down that he was doing the right thing, but this didn't make it hurt any less for all that. "I know."

He got up from the sofa and went over to the small writing desk on the other side of the room, then pulled out a sheet of paper and a pen. If he was going to disappear again, the least he could do was leave behind some sort of explanation. Not the whole truth—he wasn't sure whether anyone would even believe him, since no one in the McAllister family had Devynn's time-traveling gift —but something that might give his parents a measure of peace.

Mom and Dad, he began, then stopped. What could he possibly say that would make his sudden departure seem reasonable?

We wanted to spend one last Christmas with you, but now Devynn and I have to leave again. Please don't try to look for us—we've gone some-place where you can't follow, somewhere we need to be.

I know this will hurt you, and I'm sorry for that. But please know we're not in any danger, and we're not running from anything here in Jerome. This is just something we have to do.

I love you both more than I can say. Take care of each other.

Your son, Seth

The note was terribly inadequate, he knew. Nothing he could write would truly explain or justify what they had to do. They couldn't tell the truth and say they were returning to the future, however. Doing so would only make his parents ask too many questions, might make Charles press them for information about his future with Abigail, information Seth knew they could never divulge.

But it was better than nothing...better than disappearing without a single word, the way he had last time.

The way he almost had this time as well.

Maybe coming back here had been a blessing in disguise...well, except for the way these jumps in time were taking such a horrible toll on the woman he loved.

He folded the letter carefully and placed it in an envelope, writing his parents' names on the front. Then he set it down on the kitchen table, where he knew it would be easily found when they came looking for him.

When he returned to the living room, Devynn was standing by the window, staring out at the familiar view of Jerome's steep, snowy streets and terraced buildings.

"Having second thoughts?" she asked quietly, clear, blue-gray eyes still fixed on the world outside.

Seth joined her at the window and followed her gaze. In the distance, he saw smoke rising from the chimneys of a dozen different houses, could imagine the families gathered inside for their own Christmas celebrations. His parents were probably preparing for that evening's dinner at the *prima's* house, Molly fussing over which dress to wear while Henry polished his shoes.

"Yes," he replied, even though he knew that was a horribly simple word to communicate the feelings that roiled inside him. "Are you?"

"I suppose so." Devynn turned to look at him, and he could see the exhaustion still etched on her lovely features. There was something else, though…resolve, maybe, or just acceptance of what had to be done. "But we can't stay, Seth. You know that."

He did know it. They'd already been here too long, had already risked too much. Every day they remained in 1926 was another day they might inadvertently change something, might set in motion events that would ripple forward through time and alter the future they belonged to. Just being here for a family Christmas he was never supposed to experience was bad enough.

And yet….

"I know," he said finally. "I just wish…."

He let the words trail off. Wishing to be in two places…two times…was impossible, and they both knew it.

"I know," she said softly. "I wish things could be different, too."

They stood together in silence, watching the afternoon light slant across the living room, so different from how the space looked in the future and yet so familiar at the same time. Very soon, this would all be a memory—the bungalow in its current incarnation, Jerome of the 1920s, his parents, everything that had defined his life for the first twenty-four years of his existence.

The thought was almost unbearable.

But as he looked at Devynn, saw the way she struggled to stay upright despite her exhaustion, Seth knew they were out of choices. They had to leave, and they had to leave now, before she was too weak to make the journey.

"How much time do you need to recover?" he asked.

"I don't know." She leaned against the window frame and closed her eyes. "Twenty minutes? Maybe a half hour?"

"Then we'll wait thirty minutes," Seth said. "And then we'll go home."

Home. It still felt strange to think of the twenty-first century that way, but Devynn was right—that was where they belonged. Where their life together was waiting for them.

Even if leaving this place behind felt like tearing out a piece of his heart.

5

THE THIRTY MINUTES WE'D AGREED TO WAIT crawled by with excruciating slowness. I sat on the sofa, trying to gather what remained of my strength while Seth paced the small living room, clearly trying to work off some nervous energy. Every few minutes, he'd pause by the window and peer out at the street, as if he expected to see his parents coming to check on us and drag us off to dinner at Mabel's house.

"Maybe we should wait until tonight," he said for the third time. "After the dinner at Mabel's is over."

"No." I forced myself to sit up straighter, even though the simple movement sent a wave of dizziness through me. The exhaustion from the failed jumps earlier had settled into my bones like a fever, making every gesture feel labored and uncertain. "We can't risk it. If we don't leave now, we might not get another chance."

He stopped pacing and turned to face me, his blue eyes dark with worry. "Devynn, look at yourself. You can barely sit up. What if something goes wrong during the jump?"

What if something goes wrong? It was a question I'd been trying hard not to think about for the past half hour. My gift had always been unpredictable, but the failed attempts earlier had shaken me more than I wanted to admit. Each jump had felt different, harder to control, as if the very act of traveling through time was becoming more difficult. During that first attempt, I might as well have been trying to grab smoke with my bare hands. The second had been worse—like being caught in a whirlpool that I couldn't escape. And the third....

I shuddered, remembering the terrible moment when I'd felt my gift slip and falter midjump, leaving us suspended in that gray limbo between one breath and the next. For a terrifying instant, I'd thought we might be lost forever.

"I can do this," I said, although my voice sounded thin even to my own ears. "I *have* to."

Seth sat down beside me and took my hands in his. They were warm and steady, so different from my own trembling fingers. His touch was an anchor, the one constant in a world that seemed determined to slip away from me. "What if we get trapped somewhere else? What if we end up in the wrong time again?"

"Then we'll figure it out," I said, trying to inject more confidence into my voice than I felt. "We've done it before."

But even as I uttered those words, I knew this was different. The other times we'd traveled, every jump had been driven by crisis or desperation, had happened almost without me trying. This time, I was attempting something deliberate and controlled...and my gift had never been very good at being controlled.

The silence stretched between us, heavy with all the things we weren't saying. I could see the struggle in Seth's face, the way his jaw tightened as he wrestled with the impossible choice between staying in his childhood home and returning to the future we'd built together. Part of me—a selfish, desperate part—wanted to tell him we could stay. That we could make a life here in 1926, pretend to be the people his parents thought we were.

But I knew better. We weren't meant to be here, and our presence was already changing things in ways we couldn't predict or control. Every conversation, every shared meal, every moment of joy we brought to Henry and Molly McAllister was altering the timeline in some small but significant way. We were like stones thrown into a still pond, creating ripples that would spread outward through the years, touching lives and changing destinies in ways we might never understand.

"Tell me about the practicing you've been doing," Seth said then. "The time jumps you mentioned before. How far have you been going?"

I looked down at our joined hands, focusing on the way his fingers intertwined with mine. "Not far. An hour or two, one time a whole week, but mostly just a few minutes." I paused, then forced myself to meet his eyes. "But those were different, Seth. Easier, like my gift was finally starting to listen to me instead of the other way around."

"And today?"

"Today feels…." I struggled to find the right words and realized it was nearly impossible to describe something I'd never experienced before. "Harder. Like something's fighting me. Maybe it's the emotional stress, or maybe I'm just tired, but it doesn't feel the same."

Seth was quiet for a moment, his thumb tracing gentle circles on the back of my hand. "What if you're trying too hard? What if the reason the small jumps worked was because you weren't putting so much pressure on yourself?"

It was a fair question, and one I'd been

pondering myself. The practice jumps had felt almost effortless, like walking from one room into another. But every attempt today had been a battle, my gift fighting me every step of the way.

"Maybe," I admitted. "Or maybe traveling this far back in time has disrupted something about my abilities. Like being this far out of my natural era is making it harder to find my way home."

"You traveled to 1884," Seth pointed out.

True, but....

"I didn't do so consciously, though," I replied. "For whatever reason, my talent seemed to think we'd get more help there rather than returning to my own time. Anyway, it wasn't anything I did on purpose. And think about it—we landed in 1947 rather than going all the way back to the twenty-first century, almost as if my magic couldn't handle a jump that big."

The thought was terrifying, but it made a certain kind of sense. My gift had always done what it wanted. What if forcing this journey to 1926 had disrupted it in some way?

What if the farther back I went, the harder it became to return?

"There's only one way to find out for sure what's going on," I said, hoping I sounded a lot braver than I felt.

Seth's grip on my hands tightened. "Are you sure you're strong enough?"

No, I was pretty much the opposite of sure. I felt like I was running on empty, my magical reserves depleted by all those earlier failed attempts. But what choice did we have? We couldn't stay here, living a lie and disrupting the natural flow of time. And every moment we delayed made the situation worse.

"I have to be," I said simply.

I stood up slowly, testing my balance, and walked to the window. Outside, Jerome looked exactly as it had when Seth and I had first met here—the bustling mining town with its terraced streets and busy sidewalks, although of course there hadn't been any snow lingering in shadowy spots back in June like there was now. In just a few hours, people would be gathering at Mabel McAllister's house for Christmas dinner, expecting to see us there.

Instead, we were about to disappear from their lives forever.

Again.

"Seth," I said quietly, gaze still focused on the street outside the window. "When we leave, they're going to know something's wrong almost at once. We told them we'd be at dinner tonight."

"I know." His voice was heavy with guilt. "I left a note. It's not much, but at least they'll know we made the choice to leave."

A note. Such a small thing to sum up everything we couldn't say. I wondered what words he'd found to explain the unexplainable, to justify abandoning his family again just when they'd gotten him back.

"What did you tell them?"

"The truth, as much as I could. That we had to go somewhere they couldn't follow. That we weren't in danger and weren't running from anything." He paused. "That I love them."

My throat tightened. It wasn't enough—how could it be?—but it was more than he'd been able to give them the first time he'd disappeared.

Before I could reply, he went on, "At least they'll know we're alive somewhere. That has to be enough."

It would have to be, because we were out of alternatives. I closed my eyes and tried to center myself. Even now, I still didn't know how my gift precisely worked, although I understood that I had a better chance of it doing what I needed it to if my mind wasn't bouncing all over the place. But instead of the inner calm I needed, all I felt was exhaustion and the growing certainty that I was pushing myself way too hard.

Well, I couldn't worry about that now.

"Ready?" I asked, and opened my eyes to find Seth studying my face intently, as if he could somehow see in my expression our chances for success.

"Are you sure—"

"Ready?" I repeated, cutting him off. If I let him voice all his concerns, I'd lose what little nerve I had left.

And we needed to get the hell out of there.

He took my hands again, his grip firm and reassuring. "Ready."

I reached for my gift, visualizing our target— December twentieth, the day we'd left our own time. The bungalow as it would be in the future, warm and familiar, with modern plumbing and electric lights and all the conveniences we'd grown accustomed to. I pictured the updated kitchen with its stainless steel appliances, the bathroom with its efficient shower, the comfortable furniture Seth and I had chosen together. Home. Our *real* home, not this beautiful anachronism we'd been visiting.

But the moment I tried to direct my magic toward that particular moment in time, I could feel it begin to spin out of control. Instead of the deliberate jump I'd attempted, magic exploded outward, uncontrollable as a river in flood. The power coiled inside me burst free, wild and chaotic, carrying us away from 1926 with terrifying force.

The world dissolved around us, and immediately I knew something was horribly wrong. Instead of the specific jump I'd intended, my gift seized control and flung us forward through time like a stone from a slingshot. I felt Seth's hands tighten on mine as we careened through that other-when, completely out of control.

Time spun around us in a kaleidoscope of images—faces I didn't recognize, buildings rising and falling, seasons changing in the space of heart-beats. I tried to regain control, to direct our passage toward our intended destination, but I might as well have been trying to steer a hurricane. My gift had become something alien and uncontrollable, a force that no longer obeyed my will.

We crashed back into reality with enough force to send us both sprawling. The impact drove the air from my lungs, and for a moment, all I could do was lie on the hardwood floor and try to remember how to breathe. The light in the bungalow was different again—dimmer, grayer—and when I struggled to my feet, I could see through the windows that many of the buildings visible from this vantage point looked shabby and rundown.

"Where are we?" Seth asked, helping me to my feet. His voice was carefully controlled, but I could hear the undercurrent of concern in it nonetheless.

No, the real question was *when* we were.

I stumbled toward the kitchen, my legs

unsteady. Everything felt wrong—the way the light fell through the windows, the musty smell in the air, the sense that the bungalow itself had been changed in some fundamental way. There was a newspaper on the table—a different one from what we'd seen in 1925, thinner, with not so many pages.

"*Jerome News*," I read aloud, squinting at the date. My vision was blurry, and it took several seconds for the numbers to come into focus. "October 15, 1935."

"The Depression," Seth said quietly. Although of course he hadn't lived through it, not with the way he'd escaped the 1920s to the twenty-first century, I knew he'd studied the history of that century, wanting to learn about all the things he'd missed. He moved to the window and looked out at the town below, his entire body tense. "Damn."

I joined him at the window and found myself wishing my vision had stayed blurry. Many of the storefronts were now boarded up, their windows covered with sheets of weathered plywood. The few people we could see on the streets moved with the defeated shuffle of those who'd lost hope, their shoulders hunched against more than just the autumn chill. Even from a distance, the town looked hollowed out, like a shell of its former self. Jerome in the 1940s wasn't what it had been when I stumbled into

1926, but at least it had seemed as if it was trying to bounce back.

There definitely wasn't any bounce in the town I saw now.

"Some of the mines must have closed," I said, remembering what I'd read online about my adopted hometown. The last mine didn't shut down until the early 1950s, but others had ended their operations long before that. "I know the Depression hit the mining towns especially hard."

Seth was quiet for a long moment, his expression troubled. "My parents would have lived through this."

Horribly, I knew he was right. Henry and Molly McAllister, who'd been so happy at Christmas just nine years earlier, would have watched their town slowly die around them. They would have seen friends and neighbors leave, businesses close, and the very foundations of their community crumble away. And they would have done it while still grieving their lost son.

"The mercantile," Seth said, his expression even more strained...if that was possible. "It would still be here, wouldn't it?"

I understood his concern, but I guessed that was one thing he didn't have to worry about. McAllister Mercantile had survived two World Wars, the Depression, and the closure of the United Verde. The clan wouldn't give up such a visible sign of its presence in Jerome, even though a lot of McAllisters had relocated down the hill to Cottonwood or to even more far-flung places like Payson and Prescott.

Before I could respond and give Seth the reassurance he so obviously needed, the world lurched again, and I reached out to grab his hands, knowing if I didn't do so, we'd be forever separated. My gift had apparently decided one jump wasn't enough, and without any conscious effort on my part, we were torn away from 1935 and flung forward through time once more.

This time, the sensation was different, possibly less violent but even more disorienting. We were being pulled through a tunnel made of mirrors, each reflection showing a different moment in time. I caught glimpses of Jerome changing around us—scaffolding surrounding structures being restored, streets being paved and repaved, the slow transformation from mining town to tourist destination playing out in fast-forward.

This landing was gentler, but when I looked around, I could tell we'd moved farther into the future. The bungalow looked different – the kitchen had been updated with avocado green appliances that screamed 1960s, and a beaded curtain covered the entrance to the home's one short hallway. Music drifted through the open windows, along with voices and laughter.

"What now?" Seth asked, frustration mixing with fascination in his tone.

I made my way to the window and peered out, my legs still shaky from the uncontrolled jump. The streets were full of people—people who seemed to be in their twenties mostly, with long hair and colorful clothes that would have scandalized the residents of 1926 Jerome. A guy around Seth's age, his long blond hair pulled back in a ponytail, stood on the corner and played a guitar, and the scent of something that definitely wasn't tobacco drifted up from the street below. Bright painted signs advertised art galleries and craft shops, and I could see people carrying canvases and pottery.

"Maybe the late 1960s?" I said, making an educated guess based on the clothes the people were wearing and the song the guy had been playing on his guitar, which sounded like a stripped-down version of "White Rabbit." "The hippie era," I added, since Seth still looked blank. Yes, he'd studied the history of the town, but he probably hadn't spent much time on the '60s. "Jerome became some kind of artists' colony back then."

"Artists' colony?" Seth repeated as he came to stand beside me. He shook his head. "This is so different from what I remember."

"Different" was an understatement. The

Jerome of the late '60s had been transformed into something that bore little resemblance to the mining town Seth had known. The buildings were the same—you could still see the bones of the old structures beneath the colorful paint and hand-lettered signs—but everything else was utterly changed.

"The McAllisters are still here, though," I said, hoping I sounded at least a little encouraging. "Obviously, all this happened way before I was born, but from what I've read, it sounds as if some of them hung on and then made friends with the civilians who came here in the 1960s. That's part of the reason why the nonmagical residents of Jerome know who we are. The trust goes way back."

And was unique among all the witch clans, at least as far as I'd been able to tell.

But then, Jerome always had been a law unto itself.

Before I could say anything else, my wayward gift kicked in again, and once again, I grabbed Seth's hands. At the same time, I tried to fight the magic, to regain some measure of control over our temporal journey. I hammered my will against the chaotic force that had taken over my abilities, trying to wrestle it back under my command. But I was too weak, too exhausted, and the effort only seemed to make the jump more violent.

The world spun around us in a nauseating whirl of color and sensation. Seth's grip on my hands tightened as we were pulled through another temporal tunnel, this one lined with what looked like television screens showing rapid-fire images of Jerome's continued evolution. I saw the 1970s and early 1980s flash by in a blur of change and development, the town's slow transformation from hippie haven to legitimate tourist destination.

We landed hard in what looked like the late 1980s, judging by the cars parked on the street and the clothes worn by the tourists—and there were definitely tourists now, people with cameras and guidebooks, wandering through Jerome and pointing and gawking as if it were some kind of historical Disneyland. The bungalow around us had been updated again, although the ghastly white trim remained. Now everything had been done in Southwest colors of peach and teal, a combination I thought clashed in a particularly hideous way with the Craftsman architecture of the home.

Well, no one had consulted me on the decor.

"Tourism boom," I managed. My knees might as well have been made of rubber, and I struggled to stay on my feet. My vision had started to blur around the edges, and a constant ringing in my ears made it hard to concentrate.

"Devynn, you need to stop this," Seth said, even as he continued to grip my hands, his desperate grasp a reminder that we had to stay connected no matter what else happened. "You're going to kill yourself."

"I can't stop it," I told him. The words came out in a hoarse whisper, and I coughed. "It's not under my control anymore."

That truth terrified me. My gift had always been unpredictable, but it had never completely taken over like this. The power that had once been a part of me now seemed alien and hostile, as if it were trying to tear itself free from my body entirely.

"Then we need to find a way to ride it out," Seth said, his voice grim. "Can you tell where it's taking us next?"

I closed my eyes and tried to get some sense of what the time-travel magic wanted, but any true connection I'd once had with it seemed to have vanished. All I could sense was movement, the dizzying sensation of being pulled through time toward some unknown destination. The inside of my head might as well have been static on an old television, all white noise and chaotic interference.

"I don't know," I said. "Somewhere farther in the future than 1926, but I can't tell how far."

The world blurred around us again, and this time when we landed, I collapsed completely. My knees hit the hardwood floor of the bungalow, and for a moment, all I could do was try to breathe through the waves of nausea and exhaustion that washed over me. My whole body was wrung out, as if someone had taken all my energy and twisted it like a wet towel.

"Devynn!" Seth was beside me immediately, his hands gentle as he helped me sit up. "Stay with me. Don't pass out."

I forced my eyes open and looked around, even though my vision swam with exhaustion. The bungalow was different again, and I recognized the furnishings at once—that annoyingly busy blue and green flowered couch, the angular coffee table that sat in front of it. Matching curtains at the windows, and all the lovely mahogany woodwork covered up with off-white paint.

"I think we're in the '40s again," I said, glad that I sounded reasonably normal despite feeling as if I could go to sleep and not wake up for a hundred years.

Maybe that would be the simplest solution to our problem.

Seth glanced around. "Sure looks like it to me," he replied. "But when, exactly? We knew it looked like this when we landed here in 1947, but I don't think we ever found out for sure when the woodwork got painted over."

Good question. When we showed up on that Halloween afternoon in 1947, we'd been so preoccupied with figuring out how to get Ruby back after she was kidnapped by Jasper Wilcox, the Wilcox *primus* of the time, that we hadn't really stopped to ask questions about the bungalow's decor. And since we knew the little house had been empty for a while, I doubted there were any personal items inside that would help us identify the date, like letters or even a calendar.

"Well, we'll figure it out," I said. "Based on the way the house looks, I think we're in the right general area. Time-wise, anyway."

"You should sit down," he told me after taking a good look at my face. "Let me get you some water."

Yes, that sounded like a very good idea. The utilities had been on when Seth and I stayed here in 1947, so I had to hope the family had kept things running despite the bungalow standing empty for so long.

He went into the kitchen, and a moment later, I heard the reassuring sound of water pouring into a glass. So at least we didn't have to worry about not having water and electricity.

Not that I planned on staying here any longer than strictly necessary.

Seth came back into the living room and pressed the glass of water into my hands. Face still tense, he said, "You can't keep doing this. Each jump has been worse than the last."

That was an understatement. Those uncontrolled jumps had been far more draining than anything I'd ever experienced before, and now I felt almost empty, as if something essential had been burned out of me.

I could only hope it hadn't been burned away forever.

"I do need to rest," I admitted, then took a careful sip of water. Even that simple action required concentration so I wouldn't dribble the liquid all down my chin. "Maybe an hour or two. Then I can try again."

"No." Seth's voice was firm enough that I knew there wasn't much point in arguing with him. "Not until you've recovered properly. A few hours isn't going to be enough."

I wanted to protest, but even just sitting there on the sofa seemed to take most of my remaining strength. The thought of attempting another jump anytime soon made nausea roil my stomach. No, my body was telling me in no uncertain terms that I'd pushed it far beyond its limits, and ignoring those warnings would be foolish...if not fatal.

"How long, then?" I asked, even though I dreaded the answer.

"I don't know. Days, maybe. However long it takes."

No way. We couldn't stay in 1947…or whenever we were…for days. We could have already disrupted the timeline enough with our brief Christmas visit to 1926. Staying longer might make things worse, create more ripples that could cascade through the years and possibly change the future we'd worked so hard to create for ourselves.

"Seth, we can't—"

He cut in at once. "We can, and we will." He sat down beside me and took my hands again, his touch gentle but at the same time unyielding. "Look at yourself, Devynn. You're barely conscious. If you try to jump again now, you might not survive."

The fear in his voice was unmistakable, and it scared me more than my own exhaustion. Seth had always been the steady one, the one who stayed calm in a crisis. He'd faced down bootleggers and villainous Wilcoxes and magical amulets without losing his composure. If he was worried enough now to let it show like this….

"What if we change something?" I asked, voicing the fear that wouldn't leave my mind. "What if our being here affects our timeline in the future?"

"Then we'll deal with it," he said. "But I'm not

going to let you kill yourself trying to get us home."

I understood his logic, but the possible ramifications of our remaining here for longer than a few minutes or even a few hours still terrified me. We'd already seen how much damage one person could do by being in the wrong time – all you had to do was look at what Jasper Wilcox had almost accomplished in 1947, thanks to the way we'd distracted the McAllister clan with our unexpected arrival, giving him a chance to snatch Ruby away in a kidnapping that had been foiled in what I thought of as the real timeline, the true one. We were complete anachronisms, walking contradictions who had no business being in 1947 again.

What would we screw up this time?

But as I sat there, feeling the exhaustion settle into my bones like lead, I had to admit that Seth was right. Another jump attempt right now would probably kill me, and if I died, he'd be trapped in the 1940s forever. At least if we stayed for a few days, there was a chance I could recover enough to get us home.

"Just a day or so," I said, trying to convince myself as much as him. "Only until I can get my strength back."

"Rest," Seth said softly. "I'll figure out everything else."

I felt him adjust one of the spare pillows on

the sofa behind my head, heard him walking around the bungalow, but it all seemed to be happening from a great distance. Sleep pulled at me with the relentless tug of a black hole, and despite my fears about staying in the wrong time, I couldn't fight it anymore.

Through half-closed eyes, I saw him standing by the window, looking out at the Jerome of the 1940s with an expression I couldn't quite read. Worry, certainly, but something else, too. Something that looked almost like resignation, as though he was telling himself that we would stay here forever if that was what it took to keep me from killing myself as I tried to get us back to the twenty-first century.

The last thing I remembered was wondering if we'd ever make it home, or if we were doomed to be temporal refugees forever, jumping from one time to another without ever finding our way back to where…to when…we belonged.

The darkness took me before I could find an answer.

6

IF IT WEREN'T FOR THE WAY DEVYNN'S CHEST rose and fell while she slept, Seth would have feared that she actually had succumbed to the over-exertions of all those time jumps. She looked so horribly pale, the usual pink in her cheeks nowhere to be found.

All she needs is rest, he reassured himself.

He just wasn't sure whether he believed those inner words.

At least they wouldn't have to worry about anyone disturbing them here. His cousin Margie was long gone, and it didn't look as if anyone had designs on the apparently empty bungalow, even though someone clearly had been coming in to keep it clean. Because of that, Seth was pretty sure that he and Devynn would be able to camp out here for as long as necessary…or at least until the caretaker came by to sweep and dust.

They'd need food, though, and at least one change of clothes if they were going to be in 1948…or whenever this was…for anything longer than a few hours. But he wouldn't leave Devynn alone, and since they'd eaten a big meal in 1926 not too long before they'd left, he knew he wouldn't need to go foraging any time terribly soon.

Besides, while he might not have been as wrung out as she was, he knew all those jumps in time had exhausted him as well.

Might as well take a seat in the armchair near the couch, close enough so he would be right there when she awoke. He didn't want to sit down on the opposite end of the sofa, worried that even the slightest movement might wake her.

So he settled himself in the chair, and he shut his eyes. Just for a minute or two, just long enough so he could try to give himself a few minutes of quiet.

And then he was gone.

He awoke to find pale morning light trying to push its way past those obnoxious blue and green curtains in the bungalow's living room, and for

just a second or two, he couldn't remember where
—or when—they were. Those curtains helped to
ground him, though, and then the events of the
previous day came flooding back...the failed
jumps, Devynn's collapse, their arrival in what
certainly seemed to be the late 1940s.

He shifted in the chair that had been his bed
the night before so he could check on Devynn,
who was still curled up on the sofa where she'd
fallen asleep. Her color looked better, not as
flushed and rosy as he would have liked, but no
longer the alarming gray pallor that had frightened him so badly when they first arrived here.
Her breathing was deep and even, and when he
got up from the chair—pausing for a second to
rub his stiff neck—so he could lean down and
touch the back of his hand to her forehead, her
skin felt cool and normal.

Since it seemed as if she was still sound asleep,
he tried to be as quiet as possible as he made his
way to the kitchen to see what he could find there.
Whoever had been maintaining the bungalow
seemed to have kept it well-stocked with basic
supplies...coffee, canned goods, even a bag of
flour and another of beans. Either his cousin
Margie was still checking on the place occasionally, or someone else in the clan had taken over
that responsibility.

He put coffee on to brew and stood at the

kitchen window, which looked southward on the quiet street. Although he didn't claim to be an expert, the cars he saw parked there certainly seemed similar to the ones he'd seen when he and Devynn had been here in 1947, so he thought they must have arrived sometime close to that date.

It was strange, being back in a time so close to his own era and yet knowing he didn't belong here. The houses looked familiar, but he was acutely aware that this wasn't his world anymore. He was a visitor now, a tourist in the past.

The coffee finished brewing just as he heard Devynn stirring in the living room. When he returned, a cup in either hand, she was sitting up and looking around with a slightly bewildered expression, as if she wasn't completely sure of where she was.

"How do you feel?" he asked as he settled himself beside her on the sofa.

"Better." She accepted the coffee—sending him a look of utter gratitude as she did so—and took a careful sip. "Much better, actually. Like myself again." She paused, then added with a rueful smile, "Well, mostly like myself, anyway. I still feel a little out of it, but nothing like yesterday."

Seth studied her face, glad to see that the smudges of exhaustion around her eyes had faded and her cheeks had almost regained their normal color. "That's good," he said, and hoped she could hear the relief in his voice.

"What time is it?"

He checked his pocket watch. "Just past nine in the morning. You slept for almost fourteen hours."

"No wonder I feel human again." Devynn stretched, wincing slightly as she seemed to realize her neck was stiff…probably almost as much as his was. "Sleeping on a sofa isn't exactly comfortable," she added, "but I don't think I would have cared if I'd been lying on a bed of nails."

"Do you think you're strong enough to explore a little?" Seth asked. "I'd like to figure out exactly when we are, and maybe see if we can find any of the family."

Devynn nodded. "I think so. As long as we don't have to do any more time jumping for a while."

"No more jumping," Seth assured her. "Not until you're completely recovered."

They took their time getting ready, using the updated 1940s bathroom and getting into their last change of clean clothes—which he knew would be almost as anachronistic in this decade as they'd been in the twenty-first century—and he was encouraged by how much more like herself

Devynn seemed today. Maybe all she'd needed after all was a decent night's sleep.

The morning air was warm but still pleasant as they made their way up toward Main Street. This Jerome had a different feel from the bustling mining town Seth remembered from 1926, but it wasn't the desolate place they'd glimpsed in their brief stop in the 1930s, either. There was life here, people going about their business, even if the town had clearly seen better days.

McAllister Mercantile was still there, Seth was relieved to see, and had the same sign with the angular lettering above the door that he'd noticed in 1947. Through the windows, he saw movement inside—someone working, tending to customers. Maybe it wasn't quite as bustling as the shop his parents and brother had managed back in the '20s, but, like Jerome itself, the place appeared to be hanging on.

"Should we go in?" Devynn asked.

Seth hesitated. Part of him desperately wanted to see the store again, to walk through the aisles he'd known so well and possibly speak to whoever was running it now. At the same time, though, he couldn't help worrying about any complications that might arise if he gave in to that impulse. What if they started asking questions he couldn't answer?

After all, time travel was a tricky thing. He

wanted to believe this was the same timeline where they'd saved Ruby McAllister from Jasper Wilcox's clutches and where everyone knew about Devynn's peculiar gift, but he didn't know that for sure.

"Let's see who's there first," he said after a long pause. They'd been standing on the sidewalk opposite the store, close enough to see something of what was going on inside but not so close that he'd been able to tell for sure who was working at the shop.

Devynn nodded, and together they crossed the street and approached the big plate-glass window so they could peer into the store and get the lay of the land. Inside, Seth saw a young man —probably in his early teens—working behind the counter. He had dark blond hair and blue eyes, and seemed halfway familiar.

"Is that...?" Devynn began, then paused. She hadn't met Arthur, Seth's nephew, during the brief time they'd spent in 1947 Jerome, but of course she'd known of his existence.

"I think so." The boy was taller than he'd been during their last visit, and something about his face had grown a little leaner, showing signs of the man he would become one day.

A day Seth would never see, because with any luck, he and Devynn would be back in the twenty-first century by then.

She reached over to give his hand a squeeze. "It's going to be okay."

Was it?

At any rate, they couldn't stand out here on the sidewalk all day, or they might as well have just remained holed up in the bungalow. A bell jingled as they pushed open the door, and Arthur looked over at them, his eyes widening in shock.

"Uncle Seth? But I thought—" His voice cracked on the last syllable, although Seth wasn't sure whether that was because of stress or because the boy's voice had begun to change. "I mean, my dad said he didn't think you'd ever be back."

Neither had Seth. By necessity, he hadn't said a whole lot to Arthur during their one and only meeting, but it seemed that Charles must have told his son something about his uncle's time-traveling adventures. That was both a relief and a worry—a relief because they wouldn't have to invent a cover story to explain their presence here, but also a worry because Seth had no idea how much Arthur knew or how he'd react to the full truth, that his uncle had decided the future was the place for him, leaving his family behind.

"It's complicated," Seth said, and hoped he could leave matters there.

"I suppose it is." Arthur came around the counter, and once again, Seth was struck by how tall he'd gotten. The boy he remembered was now nearly as tall as Seth himself. "And sort of crazy, too, I suppose. Time travel seems like something out of those science fiction stories Cousin Freddie likes to read."

"It feels that way to us sometimes, too," Devynn said with a wry smile.

Arthur grinned at her in response. He didn't resemble either of his parents all that much except in coloring, and in fact, reminded Seth more of photos he'd seen of his father when Henry was that age. "I bet it does." He paused there, the grin fading. "A lot has changed since you were here last fall."

Ah, so that was how long it had been. Nearly a year. "Changed how?" Seth asked.

Arthur's expression grew downright somber. "Well, Mom passed away last month. She'd been sick for a long time, but it was still hard, you know? And Ruby was married just a few months before then—to Patrick McAllister, from Payson. He's a cousin, but you wouldn't have met him, of course."

Abigail was dead. Seth did his best to process that information, to try to determine how he even felt about the news of her passing. She'd never been particularly warm to him—well, at least not after she realized he wouldn't be her consort—and she'd been even less friendly to Devynn. But she'd still been family, and even though he'd known she would die young and pass the *prima* mantle to Ruby when her heir was still in her early twenties, it was still something of a blow to come face to face with that reality.

"I'm sorry to hear about your mother," he said quietly.

Arthur nodded, his friendly features very solemn. "It was peaceful at the end. And honestly, I think she was ready. She'd been in pain for my whole life, really." He brightened a little as he added, "But Ruby getting married has been great for everyone. Patrick fits right in, and they're very happy. She's really come into her own as *prima*."

Seth couldn't quite hold back a surge of curiosity after hearing that comment. He'd always wondered what Ruby would be like as *prima*—the stories about her in the McAllister clan made her sound almost legendary—and now it seemed he might have a chance to find out. "Do you think she'd want to see us?"

"Are you kidding?" Arthur chuckled. "Ruby's been hoping you'd come back ever since you left. She said she had a feeling your story wasn't over yet."

That sounded like something Ruby would say. Seth found himself looking forward to seeing her again, to discovering what kind of leader she'd become.

"And your father?" Seth asked, knowing it

would sound odd not to inquire after his brother. The Goddess only knew that Charles's relationship with Abigail had been complicated at best, but losing the person you'd been with for several decades still had to be difficult. "How is Charles?"

Arthur's expression became more strained. "He's managing, I suppose. Mother's death hit him hard, even though everyone knew it was coming. He's been spending more time down in Cottonwood, working with some of our cousins who moved there after it became obvious that the mines weren't going to stay open forever. I think being here in Jerome reminds him too much of everything he's lost."

Seth nodded. Charles had lost his wife, his brother had disappeared mysteriously, and his hometown had almost died around him. No wonder he might want to escape to a place that held fewer painful memories.

"But we live in the apartment over the store— Ruby got the *prima* house up on Paradise Lane, of course—and he still spends a lot of time here," Arthur continued. "Some of the cousins help out while I'm in school, but I try to be at the store as much as I can. It's good experience for me, since Father said I'll officially inherit the place when I turn twenty-one."

"You're doing a fine job," Seth said, although

he reflected that it seemed as if Charles expected a lot of a boy who was barely fourteen.

Then again, Charles and Seth had worked in the store from the time they were twelve. Not full-time, of course, but they were there after school and on the weekends, and longer than that during the summer. Child labor laws had been very different in the past from what they were in the twenty-first century.

"Thanks, Uncle Seth. That means a lot coming from you." Arthur paused, then asked, "How long are you planning to stay this time?"

"We're not sure yet," Devynn answered. "It depends on a few things."

"Well, I hope it's long enough for everyone to see you." Arthur moved toward the door. "Actually, why don't I walk you up to Paradise Lane? I was planning to close for lunch anyway, and I know Ruby would want to see you as soon as possible."

Seth exchanged a glance with Devynn, who nodded. "That would be wonderful," he said.

Arthur flipped the sign on the door to "Closed" and then held it open so his unexpected visitors could step outside. Even during the brief time they'd been inside the store, the temperature had risen by several degrees, and off in the distance, the familiar shapes of thunderheads had begun to build up above the Mogollon Rim to the east. Summer, then, and probably late summer, from the general feel of the air and the angle of the sunlight. "Come on, then," Arthur said. "Let's go surprise the *prima*."

As they walked, Seth looked around them with interest. The houses appeared much the same as they had in 1947, but a few more had begun to show signs of neglect—peeling paint and overgrown gardens, giving the general impression of a community that had seen better days. Still, there were signs of life…people watering their flowerbeds or hanging the wash from clotheslines in their backyards…and he was glad to see that not everyone had abandoned Jerome yet.

The Victorian house where Abigail had lived didn't look at all different. It was the same white with green trim that it had always been—and always would be, since it sported that same color scheme in the twenty-first century, even though the interior had been updated quite a bit. The roses in the front yard appeared especially exuberant, though, each bush so studded with blooms that it was hard to see the greenery beneath. And their scent hung in the warm, slightly humid air, lush and pure at the same time.

"Ruby's got quite the green thumb," Arthur said, appearing to notice the admiring way Seth and Devynn looked at the garden as they made their way up the front walk. "I don't think growing things was her original talent, but you'd never know that from looking at her roses."

As their little group approached the front door, Seth could hear voices drifting through the open windows—what sounded like an animated conversation punctuated by occasional laughter. It was a startling contrast to the subdued, almost funereal atmosphere that had pervaded the house during Abigail's time as *prima*.

Arthur knocked, and the voices inside paused. A moment later, the door opened to reveal Ruby McAllister. She seemed even more vibrantly beautiful than he remembered, her strawberry blonde hair now a bit longer but still styled in the soft curls she'd sported in 1947, and she wore a simple blue summer dress and a pair of sandals, showing off bright red toenails.

"Arthur!" she exclaimed. "I wasn't expecting to see you today." But immediately her gaze moved to Seth and Devynn, and her expression shifted to one of delighted recognition. "Oh, my stars. Look what the wind blew in!"

"Hello, Ruby," Seth said, finding himself smiling in response to the sudden flash of her red-lipped grin. There was something about Ruby McAllister that made everyone around her instantly more cheerful.

"Seth McAllister, you haven't aged a day," Ruby said, stepping forward to embrace him.

"And Devynn, you look wonderful. Come in, come in! Patrick will be so excited to meet you."

She ushered them into the front sitting room, which had been completely transformed from Abigail's time. Where once there had been heavy, dark furniture, somber portraits, and a few fussy parlor palms, now there were bright rugs, comfortable chairs, and plants of all shapes and sizes displayed on stands and shelves and on the fireplace mantel, and Seth found himself relaxing as he took a look around.

Yes, this was definitely Ruby's house now.

"Patrick!" Ruby called out. "Come see who's here!"

A man entered from the central hall that split the bottom floor of the house. He was tall and broad-shouldered, with the kind of tanned skin that indicated he spent a good deal of time outdoors. His hair was a brown a few shades darker than Seth's, and his eyes were a warm hazel, a shade that wasn't terribly common in their clan.

Of course they would never have met before this, not when Patrick hailed from Payson and apparently hadn't been anywhere near Jerome when Seth and Devynn were here during those terrible days last year after Ruby was kidnapped by Jasper Wilcox. However, it seemed Patrick must have still heard all about them, because he immediately grinned, his face lighting up with sudden recognition.

"Seth McAllister and Devynn Rowe," he said, and stepped forward to shake Seth's hand, his grip firm. "Ruby told me about your adventures and said you might come back someday, but I still wasn't sure I believed in all that time travel business until now."

"It's good to meet you, Patrick," Seth said, while Devynn murmured similar words. "And congratulations to both of you."

Patrick continued to smile as he looked over his wife. "I definitely said a few extra prayers to Brigid, thanking her for allowing me to be the lucky one who got to be Ruby's consort."

"We're both lucky," Ruby said, her tone firm, then went over to stand next to her husband, their fingers twining in a movement so smooth, so simple, it was obvious that such easy affection was already instinctual to them, despite only being married for a few months.

"Arthur was just telling us about what's been happening here in Jerome," Devynn put in. "I'm sorry about Abigail."

Ruby's expression sobered at once. "Thank you. It was peaceful, which was a blessing. She'd been suffering for so long." She paused before adding, "I know it must be strange to see us here, and Charles back in your family's apartment over the mercantile. It's just tradition for the *prima* to have this house."

"Not strange at all," Seth said stoutly. That was how it worked in the McAllister clan—this home was handed down from *prima* to *prima,* and if a consort survived the passing of his wife, then he needed to make his own living arrangements. "Besides, this house needed someone like you to bring it back to life."

Ruby smiled. "That's kind of you to say. Would you like some iced tea? I just made a pitcher this morning."

"Tea sounds wonderful," Devynn said, and Seth had to agree with that sentiment. After walking up the hill in the summery heat, he could use something to wet his throat.

Ruby led them into the kitchen, which clearly had been updated after she and Patrick moved in. The heavy, dark cabinets had been painted a creamy white, and the fussy drapes that had once blocked the windows were gone, allowing plenty of natural light to make its way inside. It was the sort of place where people would naturally want to gather.

Patrick got the pitcher of iced tea out of the refrigerator—the icebox appeared to be as much a thing of the past as the dark cupboards—and Ruby bustled around gathering glasses and a plate of what looked like homemade cookies, then guided them over to the kitchen table, which overlooked a garden as blooming and cheerful as the one out front.

"So," Ruby said once they were all seated, "what brings you to 1948? I'm assuming this trip wasn't exactly planned."

Seth and Devynn exchanged a glance, and she nodded at him, as if letting him know he could respond to the *prima's* question. "No, it wasn't," Seth replied. "We were trying to get back to our own time in the twenty-first century, but Devynn's gift has been a little unpredictable lately."

Ruby gave a thoughtful nod. "Time travel magic is very difficult to control." She leaned forward, her blue eyes bright with interest…and concern. "What happened, exactly?"

After a brief pause, one in which Seth tilted his head at her, thinking she should be the one to tell the story, Devynn explained about their Christmas visit to 1926, the failed attempts to return home, and the chaotic jumps that had brought them here and now. Ruby listened intently, occasionally asking questions to clarify a particular point here and there, and her pretty features grew increasingly worried as the story progressed.

"That sounds exhausting," she said when Devynn was done telling the tale. "And possibly dangerous, too. How are you feeling now?"

"Much better," Devynn replied at once. "All the rest I got last night helped a lot. But I'm still not sure if I can control another jump. It felt like my gift was fighting me, like it had a mind of its own."

Ruby was quiet for a moment, and a red-lacquered fingernail tapped thoughtfully on the table. "You know," she said, "I might be able to help with that."

"How?" Seth asked.

"My *prima* powers have grown a lot stronger," she replied. "First from bonding with Patrick, but also because of taking over as head of the clan after Abigail died. Everyone did their best to explain what that was like, but...." The words trailed off, and she gave a small shake of her head. "It's as if some part of me has become truly alive for the first time in my life. Some days, I feel so full of magic that I'm surprised I don't start glowing like a lightbulb. Anyway, I think I can lend some of that magical strength to you now. After all, I helped you get back to your own time once before, and I hadn't even grown fully into my *prima* powers back then. So I don't see why I couldn't do it again."

Hope cautiously awoke in him, and he glanced over at Devynn, who also looked more excited than he'd seen her in a while. "You think that would work?"

"I think it's worth trying. The boost from my power should be more than enough to get you home safely." Ruby paused there before adding with a mischievous smile, "Besides, I have a feeling the twenty-first century is where you belong. You both don't seem as if you fit in the past anymore."

Maybe that was the reason for the dissonance he'd been feeling ever since they left the world he'd made his own. "I suppose we've been focused on the future."

"I imagine you have," Ruby said, blue eyes still twinkling. "Well, when do you want to attempt the jump? I'd recommend waiting until tomorrow —that will give Devynn another day to recover fully. And it would be better to do it from some-place private, away from prying eyes."

"The bungalow should work," Seth suggested. "We're staying there, since it looks as if it's still empty."

"It is," the *prima* replied. "A few members of the clan have talked about moving in, but noth-ing's come of it so far, so we've just kept it tidy for whenever someone decides to take it over." She sipped some iced tea and went on, "Why don't I go down to the bungalow tomorrow afternoon? Say, around one o'clock? That should give Devynn plenty of time to rest up, and if something goes wrong, we'll have most of the day to figure out an alternative."

"That sounds wonderful," Devynn said. If she was at all worried about attempting another time jump, those fears weren't reflected in her expression. "Thank you. This means more than you know."

Ruby smiled at her. "Family helps family. Besides, I want you to be happy, and I can see that your happiness lies in the future, not the past."

As they all rose from the kitchen table, Arthur spoke up. He'd been quiet this whole time, clearly content to let the adults carry on the conversation, but it seemed he thought he should say something now. Voice diffident, he asked, "Should I tell my dad that you're here? He might want to see you before you go."

Seth had been worried his nephew might pose that question. Part of him wanted to see Charles again, to have one more conversation with his brother. But another part of him worried about reopening old wounds, about having to say goodbye all over again…especially since they'd made their peace the last time they'd seen one another.

"Maybe it's better if you don't," he said after a pause he was sure everyone noticed. "We don't want to disrupt your father's life any more than we already have."

Arthur nodded, although he looked a little disappointed. "I understand. But if you change your mind…."

"We'll let you know," Seth told him.

Ruby looked over at the boy and smiled. "Arthur, why don't you go on back to the store? I have a few things I want to talk to your uncle Seth about."

Although Arthur didn't look too happy to be excluded in such a way, he also seemed to realize it wasn't a good idea to argue with his *prima*. He nodded at her, said a quick goodbye to Seth and Devynn, and then hurried out the front door and down the porch steps.

The three of them lingered on the porch, the scent of roses hanging heavy in the air around them. "Seth, Devynn," Ruby said, her tone now quiet, almost sober, and not much like her usual ebullient self, "can I give you two some advice?"

He glanced over at Devynn, and she nodded, although her full mouth tightened slightly.

"Of course," he said.

The *prima* put a hand on his shoulder. She might have been several years younger than he, but he still felt very much the junior in this conversation. "Don't let guilt about the past keep you from embracing the future. You and Devynn have found something worth fighting for. Don't let anything stand in the way of that."

Seth gazed down at her, then cleared his throat. "How did you get so wise?"

Ruby smiled up at him, the familiar twinkle back in her bright blue eyes. "Being *prima* teaches you a lot about life. And love, family, home…? They're not always what you expect them to be. Sometimes you have to create them for yourself." She glanced over at Devynn and added, "And I think that's exactly what you two have been doing." Tone very different, she said, "I'll see you both tomorrow at one."

It was a dismissal, if a friendly one. As he and Devynn headed down Paradise Lane, Seth found himself pondering Ruby's words. She was right, of course. He and Devynn had built a life together in the twenty-first century, had found their place in a time and community where they could be truly themselves. That was their real home now, not the Jerome of 1926 or 1948 or any other time.

"She's amazing," Devynn said, echoing his thoughts. "I can see why she led the clan for so many decades."

"She has something that Abigail never did," Seth replied. "Something the McAllister clan needed to get through these times."

Devynn gazed up at him, gray eyes almost crystalline in the light of the summer sun.

"And what's that?"

"Hope," Seth replied.

7

SETH WAS ALREADY DRESSED AND READY FOR the day when I emerged from the bathroom the next morning, and was sitting by the window with a cup of coffee in one hand as he watched the street outside slowly come to life. The Jerome of 1948 was quieter than the bustling mining community I'd seen with my own eyes back in 1926, but there was still a sense of purpose here, one I could sense as I saw people going about their daily routines with the determination of those who'd weathered hard times and managed to remain standing.

"How are you feeling today?" he asked as I came over to join him. A second cup of coffee waited on the table in front of the sofa, as if he'd known I'd soon be awake and would need it, and I bent down to pick it up and wrap my hands around the warm ceramic.

"Ready," I told him…and realized I actually meant it. The bone-deep exhaustion that had sapped so much of my energy the day before was gone, to my infinite relief. I sipped some coffee, glad that it had had just the right amount of time to cool down, and added, "Ruby was right— another day of rest was exactly what I needed."

We spent the morning quietly, since neither of us wanted to venture too far from the bungalow in case we ran into someone who might ask uncomfortable questions. I'd been a little worried that Arthur might have said something to his father despite Ruby telling him he needed to keep our arrival quiet, but we didn't see any sign of Seth's brother.

No, we sat on the small porch that overlooked the overgrown backyard, watching the birds flit from tree to tree and the butterflies alight on the wildflowers growing there. Off in the distance, we could hear the distant sounds of daily life in a town that was learning to survive in a changed world.

It was strange, this sense of being suspended between times. We were visitors here, temporary residents in a world that wasn't quite our past and definitely wasn't our future. I found myself studying every detail—the way the morning light warmed and grew brighter as the sun rose, picking out every flaw in the weathered wooden siding of the house to one side of us, the tinny sound of a radio playing a song I actually recognized, something that had made an appearance in the movie *Moulin Rouge*—a favorite of my mother's, probably because of all the bustle dresses—although I'd never heard the original version before.

They say he wandered far...very far...over land and sea....

I couldn't help smiling. Yes, the man who sat next to me on the porch had traveled very far, although in time rather than space.

All of this—the half-familiar music, the houses whose outlines I recognized but were very much changed in my time, even the occasional backfire from a car as it drove up the street out front—all of it would be nothing more than memory very soon.

If we succeeded, of course.

"Worried?" Seth asked me, after we'd finished a simple lunch of canned soup and crackers and had washed the dishes by hand. We'd both been quiet during the modest meal, as though each of us needed some time to sit with our thoughts before Ruby arrived.

I leaned against the butcher-block kitchen counter and crossed my arms as I considered his question. "Maybe a little," I said. "Not about the jump itself so much—I trust Ruby completely, and even though we don't have the amulet to help us this time, I know she's much stronger now that she's the *prima* and not just the *prima*-in-waiting. I suppose I was thinking about what comes after the jump. About going back to our regular lives after everything that's happened."

Actually, I thought it was more than that, even though I wasn't quite sure how to articulate the thoughts and feelings that had surfaced in my brain. These past few days had changed something in the way Seth and I interacted, and I was still trying to put my finger on exactly what it was. This wasn't the first time we'd faced the possibility of being trapped in the wrong era forever or had confronted the reality of what it meant to choose each other over all else. This time, though, something about his interactions with his parents, with his brother, had proven once and for all that he really was willing to give up everything to be with me.

"It might be different," Seth said, his tone musing. Then he leaned over and touched his lips to my cheek, a caress that wasn't intended to arouse any particular passions, but instead to show me once again that he would always be present, always be caring. "Sometimes, though, different can be good."

At exactly one o'clock, someone knocked on the front door. Ruby stood on the porch, looking radiant in a yellow sundress that complemented her strawberry blonde hair perfectly, her full lips again wearing a red that would have made an old movie star proud. Patrick was with her, and standing behind them, to my surprise, was Seth's nephew Arthur.

"I hope you don't mind that I brought them along," Ruby said as we invited everyone in. "Patrick wanted to be here to lend his strength to mine, and Arthur—well, Arthur insisted that he needed to see his uncle off properly this time."

Arthur flushed slightly but stood his ground. "I didn't get to say goodbye before," he said to Seth. "I was at school when you left last year. I want to do it right this time."

The simple honesty in his voice made my throat tighten. This boy—young man, really—had lost so much already...his mother, the stability of his hometown...and now his uncle was leaving again, this time forever.

Seth seemed to understand the weight of the moment as well. He put a hand on Arthur's shoulder, his expression serious. "I'm glad you're here," he said quietly. "And I want you to know how proud I am of you. The way you've stepped up to help your father, the responsibility you've taken on —your grandparents would be proud as well."

Arthur's eyes brightened at the mention of Henry and Molly, and I could see him straighten his shoulders after hearing Seth's praise.

"I'll take care of things here," Arthur said. "The store, my father, all of it. You don't need to worry."

"I know you will," Seth replied. "You're a McAllister. Taking care of family is what we do."

Ruby cleared her throat gently, although her eyes were suspiciously bright. "Well, then," she said, tone a little too brisk, "shall we get started? The sooner we get you two home, the sooner you can finish planning that wedding of yours."

She had us all gather in the living room—the only space in the bungalow that would really accommodate that many people—with Seth and me sitting close together on that horrible flowered sofa while Ruby, Patrick, and Arthur formed a loose circle around us. The afternoon light streaming through the windows seemed to take on a different quality, becoming more golden, more intense, as if the very air was responding to the buildup of magical energy in the room.

"This might feel a little strange," Ruby told me

as she closed her eyes, her expression already taut with concentration. "You'll sense my power joining with yours, Devynn, but don't try to control it. Just let it guide you."

I nodded, then closed my own eyes and reached for my gift. This time, instead of the wild, chaotic force that had terrorized me the day before yesterday, something warm and steady rose within the very core of my being. My time-traveling ability was still there, still mine, but now it was supported by something much stronger—Ruby's *prima* power, flowing into me like a gentle current.

"That's it," Ruby murmured. "Now, focus on when you want to go. Your own time. Your *real* home."

I pictured our bungalow as it existed in the twenty-first century—the updated kitchen with the Viking appliances we'd splurged on, the furniture Seth and I had chosen together from various stores in the Verde Valley, the warm, lived-in feeling of a place that truly belonged to us. I thought about our wedding, now only six days away in a future I'd been dreaming about for months, about our friends and family, who might be wondering where we were...about the life Seth and I had built together in a time where we could be completely ourselves.

The magic responded, not with the violent

surge I'd experienced before, but with a steady, controlled flow. Ruby's strength anchored me, giving me the stability I needed to direct the jump to the correct time. Patrick's power was there too, a warm undercurrent that made everything feel more solid, more real.

"Safe travels," Arthur said softly, and those were the last words I heard before the world dissolved around us.

I could tell at once that this journey through time would be completely different. Instead of the terrifying roller coaster ride that had landed us in 1948, this was like traveling in a well-appointed train car, smooth and steady and completely under control. I could sense the years flowing past us—1949, 1950, the decades rolling by one after the other—but there was no chaos, no sense of being out of control.

Ruby's power guided us unerringly toward our target, and when we finally began to slow, I knew with absolute certainty that we were approaching exactly where and when we needed to be.

We materialized in the living room of our bungalow, landing gently on the hardwood floors without the violent impact that had characterized our earlier jumps. The afternoon light filtering through the windows was different from what we'd left behind in her time—softer, almost diffuse, the light of winter rather than summer.

But everything else looked exactly as we'd left it… the overstuffed couch, the juniper coffee table that we'd bought because I'd admired the one in Angela's house so much, the iron candlesticks on the mantel that we'd found in Sedona, the holiday garland of fir and pine we'd gathered up on Mingus a week earlier…all the thousand and one little details that made this place ours.

"Oh, thank God," I breathed, then immediately experienced a pang of guilt for expressing relief at leaving Ruby and the others behind.

Seth was already on his feet, moving to the window to look out at the street below. "It's definitely December," he said, although I'd already guessed that, based on the garland I'd spied on the mantel and the pot of poinsettias sitting on a plant stand in one corner. We'd decided against a tree, just because we were going down to Tucson and Tubac for our honeymoon immediately after the reception, and it had seemed silly to leave a tree up for days with no one around to enjoy it. However, I supposed that seeing Aaron and Marnie Young's blow-up penguin in the front yard across the way only confirmed what we'd both been thinking. "And it looks like it snowed last night."

I joined him at the window, and sure enough, a fresh dusting of snow covered Rich Street. Not enough to get in anyone's way—snow this light would probably be gone in a few hours—but it was still good to see that the solstice had been blessed with a little weather. And if I needed any more reassurances that we were back where we were supposed to be, the cars parked on the street were modern, sleek designs that belonged to our era, and I could also see solar panels glinting on most of the rooftops.

We were home. Really, truly home.

I went to the coffee table and got my phone out of the drawer where I'd stowed it before we left, knowing that a cell phone wasn't going to do us much good in 1926. The screen lit up immediately, revealing a cascade of missed calls and text messages, but more importantly, it showed that today really was December twenty-first.

"We made it," I said, hardly able to believe that we'd really arrived where and when we needed to be. "Ruby got us back to exactly the right day. We've only been gone for about twenty-four hours."

Seth pulled me into his arms then, holding me close, and I leaned against his shoulder, breathing him in.

It just felt so good to be here with him, to know that we really had made it home.

"Amazing that she could be so precise," he said, voice almost wondering. "Ruby really is remarkable."

"She is," I agreed, then untangled our arms so I could take a step back and look at him. "How are you doing?"

He was quiet for a moment, his expression thoughtful. "A little sad, I suppose," he said at length, then hurried to add, "Not that I'm back home, of course. Only that I wish I could have shared more of their lives, even though I know that wasn't really possible. But still, I think I'm okay. I got to say goodbye properly this time, and I got to see that they were all right. Arthur's going to do well, and Ruby...." A smile, and he shook his head. "Ruby's going to be an amazing *prima* for as long as she leads the clan."

I'd already known that, but it was a lot different to actually see her in action rather than just hearing about her based on stories the McAllisters still shared. "And Charles?" I asked, knowing Seth's relationship with his brother was the most complicated piece of the puzzle.

He let out a breath, but he still looked thoughtful rather than sad or worried. "Charles will be fine, too. He has Arthur and his work... and he also knows now that I chose to leave rather than simply disappearing." Seth's hand reached for mine, his touch warm, reassuring. "And more than any of that, I know where I belong now."

The certainty in his voice made my heart lift. This was what I'd been hoping for—not just that we'd make it home safely, but that Seth would find the peace he'd been seeking.

My phone started playing "The Carol of the Bells," and I glanced down to see Bellamy's name on the screen. "I should probably take this," I said. "She must be wondering where we've been."

Seth nodded, although he looked amused at the same time. "Cell phones were one thing I definitely didn't miss while we were in the past."

What could I do except stick my tongue out at him as I lifted the phone to my ear?

"Devynn!" Bellamy's voice was bright with relief. "There you are! I tried calling you yesterday, but it went to voicemail. Please tell me you and Seth aren't having second thoughts about the wedding, because if you are, I have a very expensive dress hanging in my closet that—"

"We're not having second thoughts," I said as I grinned at Seth, who was also smiling. "Sorry about yesterday. We had to run down to Scottsdale, and like an idiot, I forgot to charge my phone before we left."

I hoped the story sounded plausible enough. We'd already let a few people know we were going to be gone for a day while I got some pampering, and although Bellamy might have been a little miffed that she and Bree had been left out of the spa day, I guessed she would also understand why

Seth and I had needed a little alone time together away from all the wedding chaos.

"Okay," she said. "As long as you're back now and ready for all the final preparations. There's the rehearsal dinner Tuesday night, and then there's Christmas and your big day on Saturday, and—"

"We'll be ready," I broke in. "You don't need to worry about us."

"I'm not worried," Bellamy replied. "I'm just trying to make sure all the boxes are checked. That's part of being the maid-of-honor, isn't it?"

I assured her it was, promised again that I'd see her at the rehearsal dinner, and then said I needed to take care of a few things at the house.

Which was only the truth. After Bellamy and I ended our call, Seth and I spent the rest of the afternoon settling back into our regular routine. We unpacked our antique clothes—which we knew we would keep, since they'd proven quite useful and would work for any vintage dance events that might happen in the future—and I checked the voicemails and emails and physical mail that had accumulated during our brief absence.

There wasn't as much as I'd feared, but that was probably because my mother was collecting all the gifts from the Wilcox side of things and would bring them down the day before the wedding. But I was glad Seth and I didn't have to deal with an avalanche of wedding-related stuff.

That evening, as we sat on our couch—our wonderfully comfortable, non-flowered, twenty-first-century couch—eating takeout Thai from the restaurant down in Cottonwood and watching a holiday movie, I realized something seemed to have changed about my magical gift. The chaotic, uncontrollable force that had plagued me for most of my life now felt almost stable, which it certainly had never been before.

Maybe Ruby's firm hand had somehow taught it some manners.

"Seth," I said after the movie was over and we were taking the leftovers into the kitchen, "I think something's different about my magic."

He looked over at me, eyebrows raised in question.

"It feels more like it's truly mine, instead of something that just happens to me when I least want it to." I closed my eyes and reached for my gift—not to use it, of course, but only to sense its presence. Now I sensed something almost steady and responsive, a wild cry from its previous near-anarchy. "I think all those jumps might have actually helped me gain better control."

"That's great news," Seth replied at once, although something in his expression still seemed slightly worried. "You're not planning to test it anytime soon, are you?"

I chuckled, then put the takeout boxes in the fridge. "Of course not. I'm perfectly happy staying in our own time for the foreseeable future. But it's nice to know that if we ever need to travel again—which I sincerely hope we won't—I might actually be able to do it safely."

"Good," he said, his tone firm. "Because I think I've had enough temporal adventures for one lifetime."

That made two of us.

The next few days passed in a whirlwind of final wedding preparations. We met with Bree's brother Shane, the head chef at the Asylum, to confirm the menu; did a final walk-through of the restaurant to make sure everything would be perfect; spent far too much money on last-minute details that probably no one but us would notice; and had a blessedly uneventful rehearsal dinner.

"You seem happy," Bellamy commented as she, Bree, and I went over the final details for the ceremony. We were sitting in Bellamy's kitchen at her newly acquired and renovated home, surrounded by a clutter of artisanal candles and silk bags and little tumbled semiprecious stones, all of which would be put together to make the wedding favors.

"That's because I am," I said, and realized those words were completely true. "I think the time Seth and I have spent together working on the wedding has helped us both figure some things out."

"That's good to hear," Bree said with a grin. "Because I've known some people who were absolutely at each other's throats while trying to figure out the centerpieces and the menu and the rest of it. If it weren't for the way we witches have to stick to our own territories most of the time, I think Bill and I would happily elope."

"So…you *are* getting married?" Bellamy demanded, gray eyes shining with interest. "When were you going to tell us?"

"When we thought it would be a good time," Bree said calmly. "We didn't want to overshadow Seth and Devynn's wedding, and we didn't want to make any big plans until we knew you'd set a date."

"Well, you can set your mind at ease on that point," Bellamy replied, and now it was her turn to grin. "Marc and I have decided on April twenty-fifth. The weather should be really nice, which is important because we want to have the wedding outside at the winery."

That sounded perfect. The grounds were beautiful, and unless we had an odd cold snap or a sudden heat wave, temperatures should be in the mid-seventies around that time of year.

"Then maybe Belshegar and I will do something at the end of May," Bree said. "It shouldn't be too hot yet."

The conversation continued on all things wedding, of course, with the two of them talking about their dream gowns and color schemes and all the other minutiae I'd already wrestled with. I was glad to join in and offer whatever advice I could…but I was also happy to know all the chaos was almost behind me.

On the day after Christmas—the day before our wedding—Seth and I walked hand in hand up Main Street to the mercantile. It was closed through New Year's, but we let ourselves in through the back door, knowing we wanted to spend a few quiet minutes in the place that had been so important to his family and would continue to be such a key part of our lives together.

The store looked peaceful and quiet without the usual throngs of tourists who choked the place most weekends. We walked through the aisles, past displays of local pottery and the case where some of Angela's jewelry was on display, past shelves of books and gourmet foods and T-shirts and all the other items that made up the modern incarnation of McAllister Mercantile.

"It's funny," Seth said as we stood behind the counter where his mother had once waited on me when I was a confused time traveler pretending to have amnesia. "This place has sort of been the constant through everything, hasn't it? Different times, different owners, but always McAllister Mercantile."

"And now it's ours," I replied, still a little amazed by the thought that the store which had once been a simple place for me to earn some spare cash had turned into so much else. "We're part of that continuity."

"We are," Seth said, then bent and touched his lips to mine. It felt somehow illicit to kiss here, in a place that was usually so public, but I supposed it was our way of marking our commitment to one another...and to the store, so it might survive another hundred years. "And tomorrow," he went on, "we're going to officially start the next chapter."

I leaned against him and let out a contented sigh.

Yes, this was exactly where we were supposed to be.

8

SETH OPENED HIS EYES ON THE MORNING OF his wedding to see snow swirling gently outside the window of his room at The Grand Hotel. He'd spent the night there at Devynn's insistence—she'd said it was bad luck for the groom to see the bride before the ceremony, a tradition that seemed to matter more to her than he would have expected from someone who'd traveled through time and faced down multiple magical crises.

But if sleeping apart for one night would make her happy, then he was more than willing to accommodate that wish.

He lay in bed for a few minutes, listening to the soft whisper of heated air coming through the vent and the distant sounds of the hotel waking up around him. Later that day, he would be married to the woman who had literally changed his entire world. Maybe some men would have been anxious or even been having second thoughts on such a morning, but none of those worries had entered Seth's mind for even a second. Marrying Devynn Rowe was the only possible thing…the only *right* thing…he could be doing today.

A knock at the door interrupted his musings. "Seth?" came Marc Trujillo's voice. "You awake in there?"

"Yep," Seth called back, then sat up and reached for the robe he'd draped over the foot of the bed. After he shrugged it on, he went over and opened the door.

Marc entered, already dressed in dark slacks and a crisp white shirt, carrying two cups of coffee. Behind him came Belshegar, also impeccably dressed despite the early hour.

"Thought you might need some caffeine," Marc said, and handed over one of the cups he held. "And some company. Bellamy kicked me out of our suite so she could help Devynn get ready, and Bill here was looking a little lost."

"I don't entirely understand human wedding customs," Belshegar admitted. To look at him, you'd never know he was anything except the dark-haired thirty-something man he appeared to be. Then again, you could have said much the same thing about Belshegar's soon-to-be father-in-law, who had otherworldly origins of his own. "But I'm told it's traditional for the male friends to spend time with the groom on the day of the ceremony."

Seth smiled as he took the cup of coffee Marc had offered him. It was a little amusing that an otherworldly being would be concerned about following proper wedding etiquette, but Seth knew that Belshegar had been working hard the past few months to fit in with human society. "I appreciate the company," he said. "Both of you."

"How are you feeling?" Marc asked as he settled into one of the room's two chairs, while Bill took the other and Seth sat down at the foot of the bed. Smiling, he added, "Any cold feet?"

He knew his friend was joking, but Seth still considered the question as he took a sip of the coffee—which was, thankfully, much better than the stale brew they'd had to endure in 1948. He still didn't know for sure how long that coffee had been sitting in the bungalow's pantry.

"No cold feet," he replied after a moment. "I've been waiting for this day for months."

"Good answer," Marc said, still wearing that same grin. "But I have to say, you're taking this a lot more calmly than I probably will when my turn comes around."

"So, when *is* your turn coming around?" Seth asked, genuinely curious. He knew Marc and

Bellamy had been talking about marriage, but he hadn't heard any concrete plans.

"April," Marc replied, and Seth could see the happiness in his dark eyes. Previous comment aside, it didn't seem as if he was too nervous about getting hitched, either. "The twenty-fifth. Bellamy wants a spring wedding at the winery."

"That sounds great," Seth said, and meant it. After everything Bellamy had been through— having her gifts grow in strange and unexpected ways, dealing with one of the Collector's minions, finding her own path in life—she deserved to get her own happy ending.

"What about you, Bill?" Marc asked. "Any wedding plans on the horizon?"

Belshegar's expression grew thoughtful. "Bri-anna and I have discussed it a good bit," he said. "The logistics are somewhat complicated. But I'm sure it will be sorted out eventually," he added, his expression hopeful. "Love finds a way, as they say."

"It does," Seth agreed, thinking of his own unlikely journey to this day. If someone had told him two years ago that he'd be marrying a time-traveling witch from the twenty-first century, he would have thought they'd lost their mind. Now it seemed like the most natural thing in the world to him.

The three of them spent the next hour talking

about everything and nothing—transplanting Marc's landscape design business to the Verde Valley from its original location in Tucson, the plot of land where Belshegar and Bree planned to build a house just down the road from Bellamy and Marc's winery, Seth's plans for possibly expanding the mercantile into the empty space next door. During all this, he couldn't help being grateful for his friends' presence. Not because he needed some kind of a distraction from pre-wedding jitters, but because sharing this morning with people who'd become important to him felt right.

A little after ten o'clock, there was another knock at the door. This time it was Connor Wilcox, looking distinguished in a charcoal gray suit, longish dark hair slicked back from his face.

"Morning, gentlemen," Connor said as Seth let him in. "Angela sent me to check on our groom and make sure he hadn't decided to make a run for it."

"Not likely," Seth replied with a laugh. "But I appreciate the concern."

Connor's expression grew more serious. "Actually, I wanted a few minutes to talk with you privately, if that's all right. As the consort of your clan's *prima*."

Marc and Belshegar took the hint and excused themselves, promising to meet Seth downstairs for a late breakfast in a little while. Once they were gone, Connor settled into one of the now-vacant chairs and studied Seth with piercing dark green eyes that seemed to see everything.

"How are you really doing?" the *primus* asked. "Angela and I have been a little worried about you. It's not every day you start over in a new world."

Seth couldn't help but be touched by their concern, even as he wasn't entirely surprised by it, either. Connor and Angela had been incredibly welcoming when he'd first arrived in the twenty-first century, treating him not as an oddity or a burden, but as just another member of the McAllister clan. Their support had made his adjustment much easier than it might have been otherwise.

"I'm good," Seth said, and realized he meant the sentiment completely. "Better than good, really. I know it might seem strange, given everything I've left behind, but I feel like I'm exactly where I'm supposed to be."

Connor gave a thoughtful nod. "You do seem a lot more relaxed than you did when you first arrived."

"Devynn did that," Seth said simply. "She helped me understand that home isn't just a place or a time. It's the people you choose to share your life with."

"Angela will be glad to hear that," Connor

replied, the beginnings of a smile touching one corner of his mouth. "She's been fretting about whether we did enough to help you settle in, whether you really felt welcome in the clan."

"More than welcome," Seth assured him. "You and Angela gave me a place to belong when I had nowhere else to go. I'll never forget that."

Connor was quiet for a moment, his expression thoughtful. "You know," he said at length, "when Angela and I first got together, we thought we were just breaking a curse. Two people from feuding clans falling in love, ending a century of hostility. But it turned out to be a lot more than that. We'd found our soulmates, sure, but we also found our purpose. Together, we created something new, something neither of us could have built alone."

Seth thought he understood what Connor was trying to tell him. "So," he said, the words coming slowly as he pondered the other man's comment, "you think Devynn and I have something like that?"

"I think you two have already proven it," Connor replied. "The way you've supported each other, the way you've built a life together despite coming from completely different times—that's something special."

"Thank you," Seth said, and hoped the *primus* could hear the gratitude in his voice. "To both you and Angela—for welcoming me, for trusting me with the store, for treating me like family."

"You *are* family," Connor replied, his tone now firm. "And after today, Devynn will be, too... officially. But I think we all knew that already."

Breakfast was livelier than Seth had expected, since his table was joined by several McAllister cousins who'd driven over from Payson and Prescott, along with Rachel McAllister, who'd owned the mercantile before Seth and Devynn took it over, and, thanks to the craziness of time travel, was also Seth's great-niece despite being almost sixty years older than he was. Everyone made sure to keep the conversation light, clearly doing their best to distract him from the upcoming ceremony.

"I still can't believe how quickly you figured out how to work the computerized inventory system at the store," Rachel said with a shake of her head. Her hair was entirely gray now, but he'd heard it had been red in her youth. "I struggled with that thing for months when I first installed it."

"Devynn helped," Seth replied. "Quite a lot, actually. I think I would have thrown the whole system out the window and gone back to paper ledgers if she hadn't been patient with me."

"That's what partners are for," said Kirby McAllister, Bellamy's father. "Taking care of each other's weak spots. Bellamy's brilliant with wine and business, but ask her to fix a leaky faucet and she's hopeless. Lucky for her, Marc's handy."

Seth smothered a grin. Somehow he doubted that Bellamy would much appreciate being called "hopeless," but he thought he knew what Kirby was talking about.

A little past noon, Seth excused himself to go back upstairs and get ready. His wedding clothes hung in the hotel room's closet—a beautifully tailored dark gray suit that Devynn had helped him choose during one of their shopping trips to Scottsdale. Some details about its cut made it somewhat different from the suits he'd owned in the past, but overall, he was a bit surprised by how little menswear had changed over the past hundred-plus years.

As he shaved and styled his hair and got into the suit, Seth found himself thinking about his parents and his brother back in 1926—a brother who would soon be getting ready for his own wedding. By now, his parents would have found his note and realized that he and Devynn had disappeared again. They would probably assume, correctly, that this time the departure was permanent.

The thought brought a pang of sadness, but not the crushing grief he might have expected. That Christmas visit had given him the closure he'd needed, a chance to say goodbye and let his family know he was choosing his own path rather than simply being swept away by circumstances beyond his control.

And really, it was enough. Because in just a few hours, he would be starting a new chapter of his life with the woman he loved, surrounded by the people who'd become his chosen family.

At two o'clock, Seth made his way downstairs to the Asylum restaurant. The space had been transformed for the occasion—candles flickered on every table, garlands draped the walls, and creamy-white and blush flowers had been used to create arrangements that looked deceptively simple but which he knew had required a good deal of work. As far as he could tell, everything matched Devynn's vision for the ceremony, and he couldn't wait for her to see the space.

Their guests were already seated in the several rows of chairs that had been arranged to face the improvised altar at the far end of the room. As he scanned the people in the audience, Seth saw his McAllister cousins, Devynn's mother and her older sister and younger brother, Marc and Bellamy, Bree and Bill, Angela and Connor. Everyone who mattered most to both of them, gathered together to witness their commitment to each other.

At the front of the room, near the fireplace where a fire crackled cheerfully, Connor and Angela waited. As the clan leaders, they would be officiating the ceremony, and Seth thought that being married by the *prima* and *primus* felt like even more acknowledgment that he truly belonged here.

Seth took his place beside Connor, his hands steady as he adjusted his tie one final time. Through the restaurant's windows, he could see snow continuing to fall—not enough to cause any travel problems, but just enough to make Jerome look like something out of a fairy tale. Perfect wedding weather, as far as he was concerned.

"Ready?" Connor asked in an undertone, and Seth nodded.

"More than ready."

The soft sound of a string quartet began to fill the room—Bree's contribution to the ceremony, since she'd arranged for some of her musician friends to provide the music. Seth recognized the melody as something classical and beautiful, although he couldn't have named the piece if his life had depended on it.

And then the door at the back of the restaurant opened, and Bellamy appeared.

She looked radiant in a deep green dress that complemented her coppery hair perfectly, and she carried a simple bouquet of white roses and evergreens as she walked down the short aisle wearing a grin that could have powered half of Jerome. Behind her was Bree, a golden goddess in her green dress. She smiled as well…but Seth could see the way her gaze searched for Belshegar in the small crowd. Was she thinking of the wedding she'd just begun to plan?

Possibly. He had no doubt he'd hear more about it at the reception.

And then came Devynn's father, Robert Rowe, distinguished in his dark suit and looking proud enough to burst. And on his arm….

Seth's breath caught.

No one else, in this century or any other, could have been as beautiful. Her wedding dress was ivory silk, elegant and timeless without being fussy, and it seemed to make her creamy skin glow in the candlelight. Her long brown hair had been swept up in a loose bun that showed off the antique diamond earrings he'd given her for Christmas, and her blue-gray eyes shone with happiness as they met his across the room.

As she walked toward him, he thought again of how right this all felt. Devynn was the woman who'd changed his entire world…and given him a future he'd never imagined possible.

And in just a few minutes, she would be his wife.

She reached the front of the room, and her father placed her hand in Seth's with a warm smile and a whispered, "Take care of each other." Then Robert went to join his wife in the audience, leaving the two of them standing together before their assembled family and friends.

"Hey," Devynn whispered. Her eyes sparkled with happiness…and maybe just a hint of mischief.

"Hey," Seth whispered back, and gave her fingers a gentle squeeze. "You look incredible."

"So do you."

Angela cleared her throat and shot them a significant glance, and Seth realized the entire room was watching them with indulgent smiles. Right—they were supposed to be getting married, not having a private conversation.

"Friends and family," Angela began, her voice warm, carrying easily through the space, "we gather today to celebrate the union of Seth McAllister and Devynn Rowe. These two have traveled quite a journey to reach this moment—literally and figuratively—and we're honored to witness their commitment to each other."

Seth barely heard the opening words of the ceremony. His attention was focused entirely on Devynn, on the way the candlelight played across her face, on the warmth in her eyes as she looked back at him. Everything else faded into the background...the other guests, the restaurant around them...even Angela's voice became not much more than a murmur.

"Seth and Devynn have chosen to write their own vows," the *prima* continued, and those words brought Seth's attention back to the ceremony. "Seth, would you like to go first?"

Seth nodded and turned to face Devynn fully, his fingers still entwined with hers. He'd spent weeks working on his vows, trying to find the words that would adequately express what she meant to him and what their journey together had taught him. Now, looking into her eyes, the carefully planned words seemed insufficient. But they were what he had, and they came from his heart.

"Devynn," he began, his voice steady despite the beating of his heart, which he thought must be loud enough for everyone to hear, "when I first saw you in that mine shaft, I thought I was rescuing someone who was lost. I had no idea that you were actually the one who would save me. You've given me more than I ever dreamed possible—not just love, but a purpose, a home, a future I never could have imagined on my own." He paused, swallowing against the tightness in his throat. "You've shown me that home isn't a place or a time, but the person you choose to build a life with. You've been my rock through every adventure, my partner through every challenge, my best friend through every ordinary day. I promise to love you with everything I have, to support your dreams, to be your constant companion through whatever time may bring us. I promise to choose you, every day, for the rest of our lives."

Devynn blinked. Her eyes were bright with unshed tears, and he could tell she was trying with all her might not to spoil her carefully applied makeup. When Angela nodded at her, she pulled in a breath and then began her own vows.

"Seth," she said, her voice clear and strong despite the glitter of tears in her eyes, "you've taught me that courage isn't the absence of fear—it's choosing love *despite* the fear. You followed me through time, away from everything you'd ever known, because you believed in us. You've given me a home in your heart, a partner in every adventure, a love that transcends time itself." A pause, and her smile grew even brighter. "I promise to love you with all that I am, to stand by your side through every challenge, to build a life with you that honors both where we've come from and where we're going. I promise to choose you, every day, in every timeline, for as long as we both shall live."

Tears stung his eyes, and he found himself blinking as well. Every single thing she'd said was true…and he'd do his best to prove it to her every day of their lives together.

Connor stepped forward then, carrying two simple white gold bands on a small silver tray. "The rings you're about to exchange are symbols of your commitment to each other," he said. "Circles with no beginning and no end, representing the eternal nature of true love."

Seth took Devynn's ring with slightly trembling fingers, sliding it onto her left hand beside the engagement ring he'd surprised her with months earlier, then spoke the traditional words, "With this ring, I thee wed."

The simple band looked perfect on her finger, elegant and timeless, just like the woman wearing it.

Devynn took his ring and repeated the gesture, her touch gentle as she slid the band into place. "With this ring, I thee wed."

"By the power vested in us by the state of Arizona and the McAllister clan…and the Universal Life Church," Angela added with a grin, "we now pronounce you husband and wife. Seth, you may kiss your bride."

Seth didn't need to be told twice. He cupped Devynn's face in his hands and kissed her softly, pouring all his love and joy and gratitude into that single moment. Around them, their friends and family erupted in cheers and applause, but Seth barely heard any of it. All his attention was focused on the woman in his arms.

When they finally broke apart, another wave of clapping went through the audience.

"Hello, Mrs. McAllister," Seth whispered against her ear.

"Hello, Mr. McAllister," she whispered in reply. "Ready for the next adventure?"

"With you?" he said, then smiled. "Always."

The reception that followed was pretty much a blur. Seth recalled that the food was amazing—of course it was, since Bree's brother Shane, the head chef at The Asylum had overseen the whole meal —and the wine was incredible as well, thanks to the way Shane had carefully chosen vintages from local wineries that would complement each course.

There were speeches, of course, from anyone who chose to stand up and say a few words, and people tapping on their wine glasses to nudge the couple into sharing another kiss.

Not that Seth minded, of course, but he was a little amused by the practice, which seemed to be tradition. It certainly wasn't anything he'd ever heard of.

As the evening continued, they danced to music provided by a DJ friend of Bree's, shared cake that had been decorated with winter flowers, and accepted congratulations and well-wishes from everyone present. Seth found himself stealing quiet moments with Devynn throughout the night—a few minutes alone on the restaurant's small balcony, a private dance when most of the other guests were distracted by chatting with one another, whispered conversations about their honeymoon plans and their hopes for the year ahead.

"Any regrets?" Devynn asked during one of those stolen moments, as they swayed together to music that drifted through the windows.

Seth considered the question. Did he regret leaving 1926 behind?

Not for a second.

"No regrets," he said at last, and realized he meant those words completely. "Not a single one. This is exactly where I want to be."

"Good," Devynn said, reaching up to straighten his tie, even though it really didn't need straightening. "Because you're stuck with me now. Officially."

"I can think of worse fates," Seth replied with a grin, then spun her around as the music swelled.

The evening wore on, and people began to quietly make their way out of the hotel, wanting to get down the hill before the snow grew any thicker. He couldn't blame them, and it was fine.

"Ready to go home?" Devynn asked as they headed for the lobby. Bree and Bellamy had already spirited the gifts away, promising to keep them safe until Devynn and Seth returned from their honeymoon.

He glanced around the Asylum one more time —at the flickering candles, the flowers, the space where they'd just promised to love each other for the rest of their lives. Then he looked down at Devynn, beautiful and radiant and utterly perfect, and his heart swelled.

"With you?" he said, echoing the words he'd spoken earlier. "Always."

Hand in hand, they walked out into the snowy Jerome night, ready to begin their married life together. Behind them, The Asylum grew quiet and dark, but ahead lay a future glittering with possibilities.

EPILOGUE

HOME AT LAST. TOMORROW, WE'D MAKE THE four-hour drive down to Tucson, but for now, we could at last allow ourselves to rest a little. My feet ached from standing and dancing in heels all night, and the careful updo the stylist had created for me earlier that day had begun to escape its pins, but I couldn't remember ever feeling more content. The reception had been everything I'd ever dreamed of…and maybe a little more, just because it was finally a reality and not merely a vision in my head.

"I can't believe we're actually married," I said as I kicked off my shoes and sank onto the edge of our bed. Thank God those heels were finally a thing of the past. They were beautiful, beaded satin with sculpted little heels, but they might as well have been medieval torture devices, considering the damage they'd inflicted on my poor feet. Then I added, since the words had been dancing around in my head all evening, "I can't believe I'm Mrs. McAllister. It still sounds a little strange."

Seth smiled as he loosened his tie and took off his suit jacket. "Strange in a good way, I hope."

"The best way," I assured him, then reached up to start pulling pins from my hair, which began to fall over my shoulders in loose coils. As I placed the pins in a little box the stylist had provided, I went on, "Although I have to admit that I'm glad all the planning is finally over. Don't get me wrong—today was perfect—but I'm ready to just *be* married instead of *getting* married, if that makes sense."

"Perfect sense," he replied, then sat down next to me on the bed. "In fact, that reminds me. I have something for you."

I looked over at him, a little startled. "Seth, we already exchanged gifts at Christmas, and our rings today. You don't need to—"

"This is different," he said, his tone quiet but intense as he reached into his pants pocket. "Something I've been saving for the right moment."

He pulled out a small velvet box, obviously old and worn with age. The deep blue fabric had faded in places, and the edges were soft from years of handling. My breath caught as he opened it to reveal a delicate pendant nestled inside—white gold filigree set with several small but brilliant diamonds that caught the lamplight and threw tiny sparkles across the walls.

"Oh, Seth," I whispered. "It's beautiful."

"It was my grandmother's," he said. "My mother's mother. Molly gave it to me right before we left 1926, when you were getting our coats. She said...." He paused, and I could see the way he swallowed before he went on, "She said every McAllister bride should have something that connects her to the women who came before her."

Tears stung my eyes as what he'd just told me began to settle in. The pendant was a link to the family I'd never get to fully know, a blessing from the woman who'd welcomed me as a daughter, if only for a short while.

"Molly wanted me to have this?" I asked, my voice catching a little on the final syllable.

Seth nodded. "She said you were family now." He gently lifted the pendant from its box, and the diamonds glittered that much more as the piece swung on its fine white gold chain. "She also said she hoped it would remind you that you'll always have a place in the McAllister family, no matter how far you travel or how much time passes."

The tears I'd been holding back finally spilled over. Well, I supposed it didn't matter now if I ruined my makeup. "I don't know what to say," I told him, then reached up to blot my eyes with the back of my hand.

"You don't have to say anything," Seth replied, his voice very soft. "Just let me put it on you."

I turned so he could fasten the delicate chain around my neck, his fingers warm against my skin as he worked the tiny clasp. The pendant settled just below my collarbone, the weight of it somehow comforting, a link to a past—to a woman—I would never know. When I looked down, the little diamonds set in the white gold seemed to pulse with their own inner light.

"How does it look?" I asked, turning back to face him.

"Perfect," he said. "Like you were always meant to wear it."

I reached up to touch the pendant, thinking of all the history it represented—the McAllister women who had worn it before me, who had built lives and raised families and kept their magical heritage alive through generations of change and challenge. And now it was mine, a symbol of my place in their continuing story. Because even though I'd been born of two different clans, I knew the McAllister clan would be my true family going forward.

"Thank you," I said, then leaned forward to press a soft kiss against Seth's mouth. "For the pendant, for today…for everything."

"And thank you for saying yes to all of it," he replied, his lips still so close to mine. "For taking a chance on us when it seemed impossible."

Another shared kiss, one that told me exactly how the evening was going to end. For the moment, though, it was enough to sit there in comfortable silence, simply breathing in our closeness.

"What do you think comes next?" I asked at length. "I mean, I know we have the honeymoon in Tubac, and then we'll be back to run the store and all the normal stuff. But do you think we'll have more adventures? More magical crises to deal with?"

Seth's expression turned sober as he considered my questions. "I hope not," he said, and then chuckled a little. "At least, not anytime soon. I think I'd like to try being boringly domestic for a while. You know—grocery shopping, paying bills, arguing about whose turn it is to empty the dishwasher."

"That sounds wonderful," I said, surprised by how much I meant those words. After all the chaos and uncertainty we'd been through, the prospect of ordinary married life felt like the greatest adventure of all. We'd played at it a little during these months we'd lived in our bungalow, but now being married would add an entirely different dimension to our relationship.

"Although," Seth added as a mischievous glint entered his bright blue eyes, "knowing us, we'll make even the mundane stuff interesting."

"I think so," I agreed. "I mean, it's been that way so far. But whatever happens, we'll face it together. That's what matters."

He reached for my hand, his thumb moving slowly over my new wedding ring, as if he was trying to accustom himself to the feel of it on my finger. "I love you, Mrs. McAllister."

"I love you too, Mr. McAllister."

And we leaned in to kiss again. I knew that outside the bungalow's window, Jerome lay quiet under its blanket of snow. Somewhere out there in the darkness was the mercantile Seth and I ran together, the hotel where we'd become husband and wife, the life we'd built in this crazy little corner of Arizona. And somewhere else, in the flow of time we'd left behind, his family in 1926 was going about their lives, carrying our memory in their hearts just as we carried theirs.

The pendant caught the light again as I shifted, and I smiled. Love really did find a way across time and distance. It had brought Seth forward to my era and carried us both safely through our adventures in the past...and now it would guide us toward whatever came next.

I had no idea what our future might hold. But I did know one thing with absolute certainty...

whatever adventures lay ahead, Seth and I would face them together, hand in hand, heart to heart, for all the days of our lives.

And that was the greatest magic of all.

The Witches of Mingus Mountain series continues in Season of Magic, *releasing in March 2026.*

ALSO BY CHRISTINE POPE

LEGENDARY

(Urban Fantasy/Paranormal Romance)

Silver Linings

Lion's Share

Trial by Fire (February 2026)

Here Be Dragons (May 2026)

VEGAS SLAYERS

(Urban Fantasy/Paranormal Romance)

Speak of the Devil

Devil in the Details

The Devil Went Down to Laughlin

Devil May Care

Devil to Pay (April 2026)

The Devil's Due (August 2026)

THE WITCHES OF MINGUS MOUNTAIN

(Paranormal Romance)

Stolen Time

Borrowed Time

Killing Time

Wind Called

Demon Loved

Christmas Past

Season of Magic (March 2026)

Healer's Heart (June 2026)

PROJECT DEMON HUNTERS*

(Paranormal Romance)

Unquiet Souls

Unbound Spirits

Unholy Ground

Unseen Voices

Unmarked Graves

Unbroken Vows

Unholy Night

THE DJINN WARS*

(Paranormal Romance)

Chosen

Taken

Fallen

Broken

Forsaken

Forbidden

Awoken

Illuminated

Stolen

Forgotten

Driven

Unspoken

Hidden

Written

Given

Mistaken

FAMILIAR SPIRITS*

(Cozy Mystery/Paranormal Romance)

Spells and Spaniels

Cauldrons and Cats

Hexes and Hedgehogs

Charms and Chihuahuas

Runes and Ravens

LATTES AND LEVITATION*

(Cozy Mystery/Paranormal Romance)

Caffeine Before Curses

Muffins After Magic

Pastries and Prophecies

Eclairs and Ectoplasm

Sugar Skulls and Specters

Wedding Cakes and Wishes

HEDGEWITCH FOR HIRE*

(Cozy Mystery/Paranormal Romance)

Grave Mistake

Social Medium

Household Demons

Perpetual Potion

Jingle Spells

Wandering Monsters

Uninvited Ghosts

Prophet Motive

Ballroom Bits

Spell Check

Brew Confessions

Charm School

UNEXPECTED MAGIC*

(Urban Fantasy/Paranormal Romance)

Found Objects

Finders, Keepers

Lost and Found

Finding Destiny

THE WITCHES OF WHEELER PARK*

(Paranormal Romance)

Storm Born

Thunder Road

Winds of Change

Mind Games

A Wheeler Park Christmas

Blood Ties

Healing Hands

Wishful Thinking

Smoke and Mirrors

MISS PRIMM'S ACADEMY FOR WAYWARD
WITCHES*

(Fantasy/Academy Romance)

Misspelled

Dispelled

Expelled

THE DEVIL YOU KNOW*

(Paranormal Romance)

Sympathy for the Devil

Charmed, I'm Sure

A Wing and a Prayer

Wish Upon a Star

THE WITCHES OF CANYON ROAD*

(Paranormal Romance)

Hidden Gifts

Darker Paths

Mysterious Ways

A Canyon Road Christmas

Demon Born

An Ill Wind

Higher Ground

Haunted Hearts

THE WITCHES OF CLEOPATRA HILL*

(Paranormal Romance)

Darkangel

Darknight

Darkmoon

Sympathetic Magic

Protector

Spellbound

A Cleopatra Hill Christmas

Impractical Magic

Strange Magic

The Arrangement

Defender

Bad Blood

Deep Magic

Darktide

Star Bright

THE WATCHERS TRILOGY*

(Paranormal Romance)

Falling Dark

Dead of Night

Rising Dawn

THE SEDONA FILES*

(Paranormal/Science Fiction Romance)

Bad Vibrations

Desert Hearts

Angel Fire

Star Crossed

Falling Angels

Enemy Mine

TALES OF THE LATTER KINGDOMS*

(Fantasy Romance)

Dragon Rose

Ashes of Roses

One Thousand Nights

Threads of Gold

The Wolf of Harrow Hall

Moon Dance

The Song of the Thrush

THE GAIAN CONSORTIUM SERIES*

(Science Fiction Romance)

Beast (free prequel novella)

Blood Will Tell

Breath of Life

The Gaia Gambit

The Mandala Maneuver

The Titan Trap

The Zhore Deception

The Refugee Ruse

STANDALONE TITLES

Hearts on Fire (Paranormal Romance)

Taking Dictation (Contemporary Romance)

Golden Heart (Gaslamp Fantasy Romance)

Night Music: A Modern Reimagining of The Phantom of the Opera (Contemporary Romance)

Ghost Dance: A Sequel to Gaston Leroux's The Phantom of the Opera (Historical Mystery/Romance)

Flight Before Christmas (Fantasy Romance)

* Indicates a completed series

ABOUT THE AUTHOR

USA Today bestselling author Christine Pope has been writing stories ever since she commandeered her family's Smith-Corona typewriter back in grade school. Her work includes paranormal romance, cozy paranormal mystery, and urban fantasy, among others. She makes her home in Arizona.

Don't miss out on any of Christine's new releases —sign up for her newsletter today!

Christine Pope on the Web:
www.christinepope.com